DOUBLED UP

DOUBLED UP

An Imogene Museum Mystery
Book 2

JERUSHA JONES

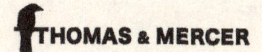

THOMAS & MERCER

This is a work of fiction. Names, characters, organizations, places, events, and incidents are either products of the author's imagination or are used fictitiously.

Text copyright © 2012 Jerusha Jones
All rights reserved.

No part of this book may be reproduced, or stored in a retrieval system, or transmitted in any form or by any means, electronic, mechanical, photocopying, recording, or otherwise, without express written permission of the publisher.

Published by Thomas & Mercer, Seattle
www.apub.com

Amazon, the Amazon logo, and Thomas & Mercer are trademarks of Amazon.com, Inc., or its affiliates.

ISBN-13: 9781477829219
ISBN-10: 1477829210

Cover design by Elizabeth Berry MacKenney

Printed in the United States of America

CHAPTER 1

The windshield wipers couldn't keep up. They squeaked rapid arcs across the glass, but my view of the highway wavered into watery columns. The entire Columbia Gorge had been blanketed by a low-pressure soaker for the past four days, long enough that even the earthworms were coming up for air and drowning on the pavement. I'd tried to tiptoe around the bloated white squiggles while splashing the short distance from my fifth-wheel trailer to the pickup, but I was pretty sure gummy residue coated the thick soles of my hiking boots anyway.

Fashion went out the window on days like this. Silk long underwear, flannel-lined jeans, thick wool socks, a thermal T-shirt, and a bulky cabled sweater puffed me up like the Michelin Man under a bright-yellow hooded raincoat. But I was warm and dry.

I turned off the highway onto the access road for my place of employment, the Imogene Museum. We'd be lucky to get any visitors today. The Columbia River Gorge isn't scenic when the bellies of dark rain clouds float just feet off the choppy gray water and hide the forested hills on either side.

I relish the solitude, actually—a rare chance to do the important, and usually neglected, curator's task of entering more of the museum's collection of random oddities into the database tracking system.

The mansion that houses the museum is by no means silent or lonely, even when empty. The old girl (built in 1902) creaks, clanks, whistles, and groans like a decommissioned frigate straining against her final anchor chain, waiting for the blast that will send her to the bottom. Sometimes I talk back, promising that the trustee board will keep patching her up as best they can.

The previous day's puddles had amassed into mini lakes splotching the muddy lawn. I picked out Ford Huckle's cabin through the spindly arms of bare oaks and maples. He lives in a converted pump house, one of the many outbuildings on the museum's sprawling acreage. I hoped the groundskeeper's new septic system could handle the rising water table. A bright-blue porta-potty still stood next to the cabin's front door, providing a shot of startling color in the otherwise drab landscape.

I turned into the paved parking lot shared by the museum, county park, and marina. A semitruck idled lengthwise directly in front of the museum, blocking the entrance sidewalk. Its blackish exhaust cloud hugged the asphalt, unable to rise through the downpour.

The white trailer was unmarked, but the passenger-side door of the dark-green cab said "T&T Trucking, Seattle, WA." Probably a long-haul driver who'd pulled off the highway last night when the rain was so hard he couldn't see. Plus, there are rules about the maximum number of hours a trucker can be on the road in any twenty-four-hour period, in order to prevent sleepy drivers from becoming a safety hazard. He'd probably left the engine running to keep the cab heated while he dozed.

As I slowed to a stop, I realized the driver must be in the trailer because the rear door was rolled up. Pieces of a broken wooden pallet littered the ground outside the trailer.

I slid my right arm into the sling that was supposed to keep my shoulder and broken collarbone immobilized, grabbed my phone, and hopped out of the pickup, pulling my hood up to shield my face from the pelting rain. I'd learned to travel light while wearing the sling because I couldn't manage the loaded purse I usually carried and everything else with one good arm. The empty right sleeve of my raincoat flapped as I trotted around to the back of the trailer and peered inside.

"Hello?" I called.

Splintered wood, broken crates, clumps of raffia-like packing material, and wads of plastic wrap were strewn on the trailer's floor. Scuff marks disturbed what appeared to be sawdust.

I couldn't see all the way to the front end, but it did look as though there were more boxes and crates farther in. Some of them might still be intact. Who would unload crates in the museum's parking lot in the middle of the night?

Unless Rupert had yet another surprise up his sleeve. I grinned.

Rupert Hagg is the museum director and great-great-nephew of the mansion's builder, the philanthropist and visionary Wilder Hagg. Rupert had inherited responsibility for the nonprofit museum. He'd hired me to do the day-to-day organizing and managing while he traveled the globe looking for items to add to the museum's roster. Maybe Rupert was in the museum, unpacking goodies.

I dashed toward the museum's front doors but skidded to a stop after just a few steps. In my peripheral vision, a rotund, person-shaped lump lay on the ground beside the back wheels of the truck cab. Yes. He'd been hidden from view when I was on the other side of the trailer.

The driver's door was open. Had he fallen out?

I gulped, trying to remember the basics of CPR from the lifeguarding class I took in high school over a decade ago.

I ran back and knelt beside the man. He looked as white and bloated as the worms I'd stepped on earlier. I jabbed two fingers in the fleshy fold between his jaw and neck. Maybe a little blip, blip, blip of a pulse. Maybe it was my imagination.

I leaned over, my cheek skimming his nose. Ragged, raspy breathing and a bitter, acrid smell. His salt-and-pepper mustache was stained tobacco-brown directly under his nostrils.

I picked up a plump hand that was surprisingly soft but heavy and limp. His steel-gray button-down uniform shirt said "Terry" on the pocket that bulged around a pack of cigarettes. Presumably one of the T's of T&T Trucking. I rubbed his hand but didn't get a response. Still, his chest rose and fell in a pretty regular cadence, and I was glad his life didn't depend on my shaky memory of CPR.

He was soaked to the skin. How long had he been lying here? In this rain it wouldn't have taken long to get that wet.

I sprinted to my pickup and grabbed the hairy old blanket that Tuppence, my hound, sat on when she rode shotgun. I winced as I wedged the blanket under my right arm, then fished the phone out of my pocket and ran back to the unconscious driver. Even though my collarbone was healing, I still felt twinges of unexpected pain with certain movements.

I flung the blanket over Terry, pulling and nudging to get most of him covered. Calling Sheriff Marge Stettler guaranteed as quick a response as calling 911, and sometimes a quicker one. Sheriff Marge was always on duty.

"Unconscious truck driver in the museum parking lot," was all I had to say.

"It'll have to be the volunteer fire department," Sheriff Marge replied. "The EMTs are in a training session at the hospital in Lupine. Get him warm and dry."

"I'm trying," I said to dead air.

He was lying in about half an inch of water. I pulled off my raincoat and spread it over him. He was too heavy to drag one-armed, and until we knew what had caused his condition, he probably shouldn't be moved.

I climbed the steps to the cab, hanging on with my left hand, and fell stomach-first onto the driver's seat. Maybe he'd have something I could use.

I scooted around until I was sitting behind the wheel. The cab was littered with crumpled potato-chip bags, empty plastic drink bottles, and fruit pie wrappers. A bobblehead Chihuahua clung to the dashboard by a grimy suction cup. It jiggled above a protruding ashtray that overflowed with putrid butts.

No umbrella, tarp, rain poncho—nothing water-resistant. I reached through the steering wheel with my left hand and rocked the key in the ignition until the rumbling engine shut down.

My foot bumped something light on the floor, and I bent to look. An inflated doughnut seat cushion, the kind new mothers sit on. And truck drivers, apparently. I tossed the cushion out the open door and eased down the steps.

Kneeling above the driver's head, I slipped my right arm out of the sling and used both hands to lift his head. I grimaced against the pain in my right shoulder and kneed the cushion underneath.

Terry moaned.

My hands came away bloody.

"Eeuww. Oh, no." I swished my hands through the puddle and shivered.

How long ago had he hit his head? The wound must still be bleeding freely for that much to get on my hands. Or else it was a deep or large wound. The puddle might have kept the blood from clotting.

I examined his face, upside down from my position. Stunted dark eyelashes. It had been at least a day since he'd shaved. He had thick, dark stubble that reached high on his cheeks and down into the collar of his shirt. The muscles in his face were relaxed, and there were wrinkle lines at the corners of his eyes and mouth and across his high forehead. Maybe in his fifties, or late forties. He would appear haggard if he were awake. Maybe it was the nicotine stains.

The weight of my wet wool sweater pressed against my back. I shuddered with sudden clamminess. Terry moaned again and jerked his right leg suddenly, pushing ripple rings through the puddle.

"Okay. Shh," I murmured, still leaning over him to keep the rain off his face.

My short brown hair was dripping now, too, and I pushed the dangling curls back, squeezing the water out.

Terry groped with his left hand, muttering something that sounded like "Get back."

I crawled around him and captured his hand, holding tightly with both of mine. He pushed, hard, and I pushed back, pressing his arm across his chest with most of my weight. Thrashing about wasn't going to do his head any good.

"Terry!" I yelled. It was like arm wrestling, but I'd sit on him if I had to. "Lie still. You're going to be okay."

He grunted but stopped resisting.

He opened his eyes—hazel, more green than brown—and focused on a spot way beyond me.

"Terry."

He squinted, dropped his gaze. His eyebrows slid in toward the center, and he blinked.

"Hey." I smiled. Water ran off my nose and dripped on his cheek. "You're going to be okay. But you're hurt, and you need to be still. Help is coming."

A tremor ran through his body. "Hit me—me—" He blinked again. "On the head."

"Yeah." I shifted. "Not me, though. I didn't do it."

"Couple guys." Terry exhaled and winced. "Came out of nowhere."

A flashing red light bounced off the wet pavement around us. The fire truck geared down to make the turn into the parking lot and rolled up to the parked semi.

I peered under the trailer and, as soon as I saw boots on the ground, yelled, "Over here, on the driver's side."

A firefighter with a medic's duffel bag jogged around and knelt beside me.

"Nasty gash on the back of his head. Was unconscious, but he just woke up," I reported.

A couple more firefighters with a stretcher appeared, so I stood and backed away.

Sheriff Marge splashed around the trailer. "Mornin', Meredith."

Her stout form was draped in a clear plastic poncho, and even her brimmed khaki hat had a plastic cover, like the cellophane wrapper on a new lampshade. I tried to suppress a smile.

"Yeah, yeah. At least I'm dry." Tufts of Sheriff Marge's straight gray hair stuck out from under the hat, and she peered at me over the tops of her reading glasses. She wore the glasses regardless of what she was doing, just looked around them when she didn't need to look through them. "You're supposed to be using that thing."

I looked down and guiltily shoved my right arm back into the sling.

"So?" Sheriff Marge asked.

"He came to just before the firefighters arrived. Said a couple of guys attacked him."

"Any idea why he was parked here?"

"No. But that reminds me. Maybe it's a delivery Rupert was expecting." I pulled my phone out of my front jeans pocket and dialed.

Rupert sounded like I'd woken him up. "Delivery? No. Wait a minute. What's today?"

I cringed at the crash as the phone hit the floor at Rupert's end.

"Sorry about that. I think—I'm trying to find—oh, well, it could be. Don't open anything until I get there." Rupert clicked off.

I shook my head at Sheriff Marge's raised eyebrows. "Inconclusive."

"The back's open." Sheriff Marge jerked her head toward the end of the trailer.

We walked to the open door and surveyed the mess inside. The trailer floor was about even with Sheriff Marge's Kevlar-corseted bustline. "Don't think I can get myself up there," she said.

"If Terry still has the bills of lading, maybe we could figure out if anything was taken."

"Terry?"

"The driver."

"Okay. Dale's on his way. When Rupert gets here, too, we'll work on it." Sheriff Marge bustled back to the knot of firefighters around Terry, who was now sitting on the lowest step of his cab with a Mylar sheet wrapped around his shoulders. "I need to speak with Terry."

"He needs to go to the hospital first, get some stitches in his head," one of the firefighters said.

"I don't do hospitals," Terry said. "Can't you stitch me up? Put a Band-Aid on it or something?"

"Nope. A doc should look at you."

"Ain't going to a hospital." Terry scowled and hunched himself more firmly onto the step.

"Well, Nick, can you patch it with butterfly bandages or something?" Sheriff Marge asked the firefighter.

"It won't be pretty."

"It's the back of my head," Terry said. "Don't have to be pretty."

"Think we could do this inside?" Nick asked.

"Sure." I hurried to the museum's large glass front doors and unlocked them. I punched the alarm code into the keypad and flipped on the lights.

Nick and another firefighter helped Terry shuffle to the men's room while everyone else dripped on the oak parquet floor and looked at one another.

"Concussion?" Sheriff Marge asked.

"Mild one, plus some hypothermia," the battalion captain answered. "He needs to get into dry clothes and take it easy for the next twenty-four hours. He'll have a bad headache for a while."

Rupert barged through the front doors with Deputy Dale Larson on his heels. Rupert, normally quite dapper, was dressed in baggy sweatpants, a black nylon Windbreaker, and loafers without socks. He did have his trademark English tweed driving cap on his head.

"Rupert." Sheriff Marge placed a hand on his shoulder and pulled him aside. "What delivery were you expecting?"

Dale and I joined the huddle.

"Statuary from Berkshire, England."

"What?" I said. "How big? How many?" My mind raced ahead to the needed display mounts and lighting.

Rupert held his hand parallel to the floor, about waist-high. "You'd mentioned wanting a children's garden, and these will be perfect. They're based on the popular illustrations by Ernest Shepard."

"Who?" Dale asked.

A grin spread across my face.

"Ernest Shepard," Rupert said. "His illustrations for *The Wind in the Willows* are perhaps the best known and most loved." He turned to me. "Kenneth Grahame, the author, loved his River Thames as much as you love your River Columbia. Different magnitude of river, but the same idea. I knew you'd like them."

Rupert's eyes shone as I bounced on my toes, hands clasped together. I'm sure I looked like a five-year-old at a surprise birthday party.

"Did you get a Mole statue?" Mole was far and away my favorite character in the delightful children's stories.

"Let's have a look."

"Hold on a minute," Sheriff Marge said. "That trailer is a crime scene until I say it's not. Dale, get your kit."

We walked outside and stood at the back of the trailer, waiting until Dale rummaged through his cruiser's trunk and rejoined us.

My teeth chattered from the cold and the excitement. I pressed my slinged arm across my middle, trying to retain some body heat inside my soggy sweater.

Dale pulled on latex gloves and hoisted himself into the trailer. Sheriff Marge handed him blue paper booties that he slipped on over his shoes.

"Oh. I know." I trotted to the cab and scanned the floor for a bundle of papers. I found what I was looking for in the pocket of the driver's door—a clipboard of wet forms with smeared ink, Terry's delivery schedule and bills of lading. I flipped through the stack, careful not to tear the limp pages.

"He had two deliveries on board—one for us and one for a gallery in Portland. Both picked up in Seattle yesterday. The booking was handled by the same freight-forwarding company that arranged their shipment in a sealed container, so they must have come over on the same freighter. Port of departure was Liverpool. Our shipment is listed as 'stone statuary.' The shipment for the Portland gallery is listed as 'carved wood artifacts.'"

"What's the name of that gallery, Meredith?" Dale asked from deep inside the trailer. He was bent over, aiming a pencil flashlight into the shadows.

I picked out the faded letters. "The Rittenour Gallery, on Naito Parkway."

"Then I think I got something," Dale said. He squatted and lifted a crate the size of an apple box and brought it to the open doorway. "This crate's addressed to Rittenour. It fell between a couple of the big crates that are addressed to the Imogene. Your crates appear intact, and there are five of them. Does that match the paperwork?"

"Yes. Five statues," Rupert said. "Toad, Rat, Mole, Otter, Badger."

I shuffled quickly. "Yeah. Five listed on the bill of lading, too."

"So somebody followed this truck, conked the driver on the head, and stole the crates addressed to the Rittenour Gallery," Sheriff Marge said.

"Except they missed one." Dale tapped the wooden box.

"There were fourteen crates for the Rittenour," I said.

"Uh-huh." Sheriff Marge stood with arms akimbo. "Rupert, would you mind checking on Terry, see if Nick is finished with him yet? Set him up with some coffee. I'll be in soon to take his statement."

Rupert nodded and disappeared around the side of the trailer.

Sheriff Marge pulled a folded clear plastic tarp out of Dale's kit bag and opened it on the ground. "Since it's stopped raining, Dale, set the crate down here."

Dale jumped from the trailer, slid the crate off, and eased it to the tarp. "Thing weighs a ton for its size."

We stared at it. Sheriff Marge cleared her throat.

I glanced at Sheriff Marge and found her ogling me with raised eyebrows. "What?"

"I think that, as the curator of a similar institution, you might be overcome with professional curiosity," Sheriff Marge said. "Especially since I don't have a search warrant on me."

Dale bent his head and scratched his neck, then strode to his squad car and returned with a crowbar. The bottomless trunk of a deputy sheriff. He handed me the crowbar. "Happy birthday."

"It's not—oh. Thank you."

Sheriff Marge turned and gazed out over the river, where the clouds had lifted a little, revealing a couple of winterized sailboats bobbing at the end of the marina docks. She whistled the same three notes over and over.

I shared an amused look with Dale, then stuck the flat end of the crowbar under the corner of the crate's lid. It came off with a sharp cracking sound. Compressed raffia-like packing material sprang up, and some tumbled out.

Sheriff Marge and Dale crowded in to watch but let me do the unpacking. I removed a few clumps of the brown grassy stuff, then jumped back. "Yah!" I shrieked.

Sheriff Marge high-stepped out of the way as half a dozen huge brown beetles scrambled over the lip of the crate, plopped onto the tarp, and darted under the trailer.

I realized I still had packing material in my hand and flung it to the ground. "What were those?"

"Haven't you ever seen cockroaches?" Sheriff Marge asked, breathing hard.

"Gross. Shouldn't they have died? In the crate?"

"Cockroaches can go a month without food," Dale said. "In fact, they can live that long without heads, too, because they breathe through spiracles. They really only need their heads for eating and drinking."

Sheriff Marge and I stared at him.

Dale shrugged. "My kid's doing a report on insects for school. Hey." He snapped his fingers. "If I can catch one of those, he could pin it in his display case."

"There'll be plenty more," Sheriff Marge said. "You ready?"

She kicked the crate and quickly retreated. An extended family of creepy monster bugs fled over the crate's sides. Dale held up the tarp edge to keep the scrabbling creatures contained. He reached in with a gloved hand and grabbed a big one. Then he let the tarp drop, and we watched the rest of the roaches escape through the puddles. Dale dropped his catch in an evidence bag and sealed it.

I shuddered. "I need gloves before I'm touching anything else in that crate."

Dale handed me a pair of gloves. I slid them on and bent over the crate, gingerly picking at the packing material. It became mustier and damper the deeper I plunged. "Phew. Water must have leaked in somehow."

"Which would have made the roaches happy," Dale said near my shoulder. He was squatting, watching closely as I pulled out a gob of reeking cockroach nest.

"I think maybe I should be wearing a mask," I said, and my hand bumped something hard. I felt around the foot-long object and lifted it, brushing off the loose raffia strands. A dark, carved wooden statue of a woman with a grotesquely disproportionate face and figure.

"Whoa," Dale said. "Thank God none of the women I know look like that."

I rolled my eyes.

"What is it?" Sheriff Marge asked.

"I'd guess aboriginal folk art. I can't even tell you what continent, but probably Pacific Islands, Australia, or Africa. If I knew what kind of wood, that might narrow down the location. It's really heavy."

"Because it got wet?" Sheriff Marge held out her gloved hands.

"I don't know." I handed the statue to her and bent to rummage through the crate again. I found seven more statues—another woman, three men, a water buffalo/cow, a goat, and a creature that appeared to be a cross between a boar and an anteater—all with body parts skewed or somehow not quite right.

"Fourteen crates of those, huh?" Dale said. "How much do you think they're worth?"

"Not much, except to a collector," I answered, "or for historical reasons. But if they're valuable historically, they should have stayed in their country of origin, which I'm quite sure is not England."

"So it's fishy," Sheriff Marge said.

"Yeah. I think the shipment was fishy to start with, and became fishier when someone stole most of it," I answered.

Sheriff Marge set her fists on her hips. "Dale, we're impounding the truck and all its contents until we can sort this out."

"What about my statues?" I asked.

"What?"

"Mole, Ratty, Toad—"

Sheriff Marge scowled. "More animals?"

"Much cuter animals. You'll see."

"You can probably have them. But I want to talk to the driver first."

"Who's getting very fidgety," Rupert said, strolling into view and puffing on a Swisher Sweet cherry cigar. "Ford's keeping him company." His eyes widened. "What is that?"

Wrinkling my nose, I held up a statue.

"Hideous."

"And the reason the truck was broken into," Sheriff Marge said. "Know anything about it?"

Rupert hunched toward the statue and squinted but did not offer to take it from me. "No. This kind of stuff has never appealed to me. A form of folk art, I suppose. Not North American or European, that's for sure. Or Asian, for that matter." He shuddered. "I wouldn't want that thing looking at me from a shelf."

"Maybe they're death statues," Dale said.

He returned a sheepish grin as we stared at him again. "Discovery Channel."

"Well, like you said, nobody wants to look at these very long," I said. "They make me feel off-balance—tilted, while my brain tries to make sense of them. So better they're buried in a grave than out in public view. Weird."

"And worth something to somebody, which means I don't want to leave them in this trailer with the lock busted," Sheriff Marge said.

"I can keep them in my office," I replied. "I'll research them. Should we contact the Rittenour Gallery?"

"Not yet. I need to get my notes in order first. But good, your office will be fine for now." Sheriff Marge pulled her gloves off. "Is the driver in the kitchen?"

"Yes." Rupert turned to walk with Sheriff Marge.

"Can you send Ford out with a transit cart?" I called. "There's no way I'm taking this crate up to my office."

Rupert waggled the okay sign.

Doubled Up

As soon as I stopped moving, a chill crept deep into my flesh, making me shiver from the inside out. I retrieved my raincoat and jammed my good arm into the sleeve.

CHAPTER 2

A few minutes later, Ford Huckle, the museum's groundskeeper and handyman, pushed a transit cart with a squeaky wheel out the museum's front entrance and around to the back of the trailer. His perpetual grin revealed more gaps than stumps of teeth.

Ford was wearing what he always wore—dirty, olive-green coveralls and mud-caked boots. Today, though, he also had a floppy-brimmed camouflage fishing hat tamped down on his head with the drawstring pulled snug under his jaw.

"Here you are, Missus Morehouse," he said.

"Thanks, Ford." I shook my head. The "missus" always gets me. I think Ford knows I'm not married. But he calls all women "missus," so I suppose it's his way of showing respect. Ford grew up in an era when kids with developmental disabilities were classified as "slow," and no one bothered to figure out why, or if anything could be done to help them.

I crouched and placed a statue on the cart's protected second shelf since it was starting to sprinkle again.

Ford knelt beside me and picked up the anteater/boar figure. He turned it over in his large callused hands and fingered the long snout. "What is it?"

"Some kind of animal, I expect."

"Not from these parts." He placed the statue on the cart and reached for the water buffalo.

"Nope," I agreed. "It's a mystery."

"You goin' to display these?"

"Not for us. For another museum. We're just going to keep them safe for a while."

"Pop whittled better'n this. Made me a Noah's ark when I was a tyke."

I examined Ford's lined face as he placed the last figure on the cart. "Do you still have any of your dad's carvings?"

"Got used for kindlin' one hard winter. I'd outgrowed 'em anyway."

I pondered that bit of information. I mourned the great loss reflected in such a simple statement—the loss of what was probably interesting if not valuable folk art, the loss of a parent-child bond held in an object lovingly made, the loss of childhood innocence when toys were burned for survival. I inhaled sharply before the dreamy past sucked me in too far—one of the perils of the job. I often find myself imagining walking around in other people's skins, looking out through their eyes, when I handle the things they used.

"Do you have a rain slicker, Ford?"

"Forgot. Goin' back to get it after I help you."

"Good. How's your new septic system?"

"Everythin' drains."

Talking seemed to exhaust Ford. I'd maxed him out with this verbal spurt—it would be a while before he was ready for another chat.

I straightened and waved to Dale, who was methodically scanning the ground in arcs around the truck and trailer. Ford followed me along the sidewalk, pushing the noisy cart. I held the doors open for him.

We rolled past the gift shop, across the oak parquet floor of the main ballroom, and beyond a maze of hallways to the freight elevator tucked next to the servants' stairwell.

We rode in silence, listening to the groan and rattle of the old cables. The elevator is original to the mansion and was quite a novelty for a private residence at the time.

At the top floor, the doors creaked open. I unlocked my office door. I sidled around my desk and stacked piles of books and papers together to clear some space. Ford lifted the statues off the cart and stood them on my desk as though he were placing bone-china teacups.

One of the male figures fell over with a loud clunk.

Ford cringed. "Sorry." He tried to right it.

"Not your fault. They're lopsided." I patted his arm. "Let's lay them on their sides."

"Thanks, and don't forget your raincoat," I called as Ford trundled the cart back to the elevator.

I quickly made copies of the bills of lading from Terry's clipboard. Then I sped down the stairs to make a detour on the first floor and, I hoped, catch the end of Terry's interview with Sheriff Marge.

ooo

Terry turned out to be shorter than I'd expected. I hadn't noticed when he was flat on his back, but now that he was perched like a gray leprechaun—knees splayed, heels hooked on the high rungs of a bar stool, paunchy belly tipped over his low beltline—my first thought was that it wouldn't have taken much to conk him on the back of the head. I probably could have managed it myself under cover of dark. Given the possible value of the shipment, it seemed odd it had been in the care of this little man. He probably didn't know anything about the contents of his trailer, though.

His eyebrows scowled into a unibrow, and his chin jutted forward. His arms were crossed over his chest and rested lightly on his belly shelf. Sheriff Marge, still ensconced in rain gear, leaned against the counter next to the coffeemaker, periodically smacking the base of an empty mug she held in one hand into her other palm.

I've known Sheriff Marge for more than two years, and this was the first time I'd seen her look fierce. Stern, in-charge, no-nonsense, don't-mess-with-me-mister? Yes. But fierce? No. Not until today.

I fought a rising urge to laugh. Here were two stocky, gray-haired adults well into the experienced years of their lives, and they might as well have been toddlers in a tugging match over a toy: Sheriff Marge "you have to share" versus Terry "you can't make me."

I slid into a folding chair next to the lunch table. If there'd been a bookie on the premises, I'd have placed all my pocket money on Sheriff Marge in this battle of the wills. Terry didn't stand a chance.

Terry finally burst the silence. "What do you expect me to do, sit here until you catch the guys who attacked me? At the rate you're going, I'll be Rip Van Winkle."

"The more you tell me, the faster I'll move. Why do you think I'm still standing here?" Sheriff Marge replied.

"I got a job to do, or I'll get fired."

"Which is why I'd like to see your CDL. No doubt your employer requires you to have a commercial license."

"They must've taken it."

"They?"

"The guys who attacked me."

"There's a bulge in your back right pocket. I presume that's your wallet. Let's have a look."

"It ain't in there."

"So you're saying these guys stole your license but not your wallet?"

"Yeah."

I wrinkled my nose. Terry was a terrible liar.

"Where do you keep your license?" Sheriff Marge asked.

"With my paperwork."

"You mean this?" I held up the clipboard.

Terry's jutting angles—elbows and knees—slumped, and he lifted a hand to feel the bandage on the back of his head. He grunted.

"This is all really tidy. Everything looks in order," I continued. "You keep a permanent document like your license with the paperwork that changes from load to load? I can't imagine how you keep from losing it."

Sheriff Marge fired a warning glance my direction.

"Well, maybe I lost it," Terry mumbled. "Don't remember."

"Uh-huh. Well, my deputy's going to come sit here with you while I get into the database and dig up your license," Sheriff Marge said.

"Uh, one thing," I said. "I need Terry to move the truck. It's blocking the view of the museum's entrance. We get so few visitors as it is, I'd hate to make it even harder for them to find their way into the building. We're opening in twenty minutes."

Sheriff Marge blew out a big breath. "Okay." She pointed at Terry. "Park your rig down by the marina, out of the way. It's staying there until we figure this out."

Terry sidled by Sheriff Marge, glaring at her out of the corner of his eye.

I waited a second and then whispered, "What'd I miss?"

"Not much," Sheriff Marge replied in an undertone as we followed Terry at a discreet distance. "He was downright chatty about the guys who robbed him. Swears there were at least two, maybe three or four, because the only way he could be waylaid is if they ganged up on him. Claims he doesn't remember anything after getting hit on the head."

I arched my eyebrows.

"Yeah, I know. Arrogant little peacock."

"But why was he here in the middle of the night?"

"Closer to four a.m. No good explanation. Just said he was early. Said he was stretching his legs before catching some shut-eye when he was jumped. He thought they'd planned it, were waiting for him."

"So they knew what was in the trailer." I caught the right front door on its swinging rebound from Terry's forceful shove and held it open for Sheriff Marge.

"Not sure how much to believe." Sheriff Marge sighed. "Especially since he completely clammed up when I started asking questions about him personally."

We stopped on the sidewalk and watched Terry stalk to the cab, climb in, and slam the door. "By the way, providing excuses for a hostile witness is not a great idea."

"Sorry," I said. "I was thinking out loud."

The truck engine snorted to life and coughed a cloud of black smoke out the high exhaust pipe. Dale jogged around the trailer and held his arms out in a questioning gesture. Sheriff Marge nodded her plastic-covered hat in answer.

Dale ambled up to us. "Not much on the ground. Looks like they opened one or two cases to check the contents, and that's what the splintered wood fragments are from. I think they took the rest of the cases unopened, except the one they missed."

"Did Terry say anything about hearing or seeing another vehicle in the parking lot?" I asked. "That crate was heavy. They'd have needed a van or pickup or something larger to haul thirteen of them."

Sheriff Marge's answer was drowned in the grinding of gears as Terry swung the truck in a tight turn to clear the curbs marking the handicapped parking spots and my pickup beyond them. I held my breath as the semi's left front fender came within a handbreadth of my truck's back bumper. Then Terry straightened the trailer and moved toward the marina at the far end of the long shared parking lot.

"No," Sheriff Marge re-answered.

"Do you think he was in on it?" I asked.

"Always a possibility."

"Hey," Dale said. "He's making a run for it."

Instead of slowing and pulling the truck to the edge of the lot, Terry turned onto the access road toward the highway.

"Maybe he's going to back into position," I said.

"I don't think so," Dale called over his shoulder as he ran to his squad car. Terry was picking up speed.

"I thought he was belligerent, but not stupid," Sheriff Marge muttered. She trotted to her SUV, poncho flapping behind, and hoisted her bulky frame into the seat. She gunned the engine and took off with a squeal of tires, the door smacking shut on its own.

Dale's Crown Vic and Sheriff Marge's Explorer converged on the semitruck, lights flashing. Terry was definitely heading for the highway.

Then I spotted bits of bright blue and yellow moving through the trees. I stepped out a few feet to get a better view. It was Ford in his raincoat, on the tractor he used for mowing. But instead of pulling the mower attachment, he was pulling a little trailer with the porta-potty strapped on it. The tractor and porta-potty plowed through the muddy lawn toward the access road.

"Stop! Ford!" He was too far away to hear. I waved my good arm and jumped up and down. Ford kept looking back, checking his trailer, not watching ahead.

The tractor chugged along at a poky pace while the semi shuddered with a gear change and charged even faster on the smooth pavement. Terry wasn't going to see a little tractor coming through the trees. My hand flew to my mouth, and I hunched my shoulders instinctively, bracing for impact.

Ford reached the access road in front of the semi, but not by much. I couldn't tell from my angle, but surely there wasn't enough distance separating the two vehicles for Terry to stop.

For a split second everything moved in slow motion—Ford rolled fully onto the road, the lights on the patrol cars swooped across the dirty white semitrailer and the gray-barked tree trunks. Then the tractor skipped sideways with a horrible crunching noise as the trailer bore down on it, the brakes—or was it the gears?—grinding, scraping, piercing, metal-on-metal screams.

Ford swerved, and his action flung the porta-potty airborne. It popped off the trailer as if it were spring-loaded, the door flapping open in flight. A corner pogoed off the pavement, and the blue hut somersaulted a couple of times before coming to a rest on its side.

The semi shimmied in little hops, then stood still, heaving and steaming. Somehow Terry had whoaed that rocketing weight up and sideways, like a cowboy jerking the reins hard on a horse's bridle, pulling the brute to a sitting stop.

I sucked in a breath.

Dale sprinted toward the cab, gun held stiff-armed, pointed down. When he came even with the door, he aimed at the driver's window. His voice carried on the damp air. "Show me your hands. Now!"

Terry's white face and two palms wobbled into view.

Ford. Where was Ford?

I charged the shortest distance, across the sucking mud, straight through lake-size puddles. My nylon raincoat swished against tree trunks as I sideswiped them. Like a running back dodging lumbering linemen and free safeties, I swerved, stumbled, but kept my feet churning.

My mud-caked boots felt like twenty-pound flippers by the time I reached the access road. I ran around the semi cab and stalled tractor, then tiptoed along the edge of the neon-blue chemical sludge that was oozing out of the damaged porta-potty. It reeked—a mixture of breath mints, orange peel, and the kind of floor cleaner used in hospitals. Sickly sweet and gross. Ford stood, arms akimbo, surveying the mess. He looked okay—no blood.

I bent in half, panting.

"Jim won't like this," Ford said.

"Jim?" I struggled for clean air.

"He told me to have the latrine out at the main road today. He's goin' to pick it up."

"I don't suppose it has to be right side up for him to pick it up."

Ford stepped back as the seepage crept toward the tips of his boots.

"You all right?" I asked.

"Got nothin' to complain about."

A giggle burbled up, and I couldn't hold it back. I patted Ford's shoulder.

Sheriff Marge power walked up to us, huffing, accompanied by the crinkly rustle of her poncho. "Injuries?"

Ford didn't answer, so I shook my head.

"Phew," Sheriff Marge said.

I glanced at her, but Sheriff Marge was staring off into the trees. Her word could have referred to the odoriferous cloud emanating from the porta-potty, or the entire morning's excitement, or plain old relief that a wreck hadn't happened.

"How's Terry?" I asked.

"Scared the hooey out of him. He'll be talking now."

CHAPTER 3

Dale and Ford stayed on the scene waiting for a tow truck and the porta-potty pick-up guy, respectively. Through traffic was impossible until the semi could be straightened and shoved to the side, and the blue seepage dealt with.

Back in the Imogene's staff kitchen, Sheriff Marge settled in for a heart-to-heart with Terry. She shed her poncho and hat and warmed a mug of coffee in the microwave. I skipped the bitter brew, but started in on the sandwich of roast beef, provolone, tomato, and peperoncini I'd packed for lunch. The recent adrenaline rush had made me hungry.

Terry slouched in a folding chair like a day-old balloon sculpture. The skin on his face hung in long folds. Even his mustache drooped. He shivered under the thick blanket I'd found for him.

The flimsy chair creaked under Sheriff Marge's weight as she eased into it. She plunked her mug on the table. "Let's start with you. Then we'll talk about the incident this morning."

Terry stared at the floor.

"Is Terry Ambrose your real name?"

"Yes."

"Do you have a commercial driver's license?"

"Not right now."

Sheriff Marge shifted, but Terry wouldn't make eye contact.

"Why are you driving a semi without a CDL?"

"Need the money."

"Terry, this will go a lot faster if you fill in for me here. You want to tell me your story?"

He spread his shaking fingers. "I need a cigarette."

"Just as soon as you tell me what's going on."

He ran a tentative hand across his forehead, then fingered the bandage on the back of his head. "I'm on parole. Got out a couple months ago. Been working for my cousins who own a small warehousing business. It was the only place I could get work with my record."

Sheriff Marge sipped her coffee and left her notebook on the table, unopened.

"But it's not full-time. It's not even part-time most of the time. My mother has emphysema and no insurance, and she's getting worse. I need money for her inhalers." Terry paused and looked up for the first time. "She's been good to me, you know, even though I haven't been good to her."

Sheriff Marge raised an eyebrow.

"A few weeks ago, the manager of the regional trucking firm next door came over to see if anybody could drive a rig. One of their drivers got arrested for a fight with his girlfriend or something and couldn't make his usual run. I've driven trucks before—before I went to prison, so I said yes. The guy offered me cash, off the books, to fill in here and there. Didn't want to go through all the HR hassle and paperwork, he said. Cash sounded good to me, so I took the job."

"And this firm is T&T Trucking?"

Terry nodded. "I've done a few runs for them. Try to drive at night and take side roads around weigh stations."

"The stolen shipment was intended for a gallery in Portland. One of the conditions of your parole is that you not leave the state without notifying your parole officer, right?"

"Yeah."

"And I assume your parole officer has no idea you're doing this cash-basis job on the side?"

"Yeah." Terry massaged his hands.

"Do you know what was in the shipment for the Rittenour Gallery?"

"Just what it said on the bill of lading—wood artifacts."

"Did you see those wood artifacts?"

Terry shook his head.

"What did you serve time for?"

"Forgery."

"How long were you in?"

"Three and a half years."

Sheriff Marge blew out a breath. "Then it wasn't your first offense."

Terry rocked forward and clasped his hands between his knees. "Third. First felony."

"You might be really lucky you didn't make that delivery in Oregon." When Terry didn't answer, she continued. "Why'd you run?"

"All that—what I just told you. Guess I panicked."

"And tried to outrun us in a semi?"

"I've had a really bad day, all right?"

Sheriff Marge's eyes were straight-shooting serious. She leaned forward. "Let me tell you something. I have plenty of ex-cons living in my county. The ones who make an effort at clean living seem to prefer being out here, away from so many people, the craziness, the stress. I have a lot of respect for them—provided they're honest. You're not rolling in the right direction. Want to give me a reason to trust you?"

Terry spread his hands in an open gesture. "That's what I'm doing."

"So who are your buddies, the ones who conked you on the head? Give me names."

Terry's faced flushed deep purple-red, and he slid forward a few inches. His eyes bulged to the size of jumbo jawbreakers, speckled and bloodshot. "I told you, I don't know them," he spluttered. His folding chair tipped, and he pushed the feet back down on the tile floor with a violent clank. "Didn't even see them. I have no idea who they are."

"Who knew about this trip?"

"Tom. Tom Hiller, the manager, and the dispatcher, Olivia. My cousin knew I was going south, but I didn't tell him the addresses."

"Just those two? You mention it to your mother, friends, bartender, anyone else?"

"Didn't have a chance." Terry's face was draining to its normal ashen color. "Tom asked me to do it around six p.m. yesterday. I went home, told my mom I was making a run but not where to—didn't want her to worry about the Oregon stop. I slept a few hours, then went back to the truck yard. Left around twelve thirty this morning."

Sheriff Marge tore a blank sheet out of her notebook, clicked her pen open, and slid both across to Terry. "I want you to think about it and write down everything you remember about deliveries you've made for this T&T Trucking—dates, business names and addresses, or at least general locations, what items were listed on the bills of lading, names of people who signed for the deliveries, anything else you can think of."

Terry accepted the pen and paper. "I need a smoke."

"Meredith'll set you up."

I snapped to attention. The museum didn't have a dedicated smoking area. I'd have to take him outside, but raindrops were still ticking against the windowpanes.

"And if you run this time," Sheriff Marge said, "you'll be on foot, alone, wet, cold, hungry. People are mighty suspicious of hitchhikers around here. And we have dogs, lots of dogs—the kind that hunt bear, coons, cougar. They'd be thrilled to go after you."

"I'm not running," Terry muttered.

Behind his back I rolled my eyes, but Sheriff Marge didn't acknowledge me, didn't let any levity slip through her stern demeanor. Terry Ambrose had definitely gotten on her nerves, and that was hard to do.

I led Terry out the narrow kitchen door and dashed to a gazebo at the far end of what used to be the cook's garden. It must have been glorious in its heyday. Among the family papers, I had found garden plans. The raised beds once contained herbs, vegetables, and edible flowers. Now their crumbled frames are overrun by a thick thatch of prairie grass and weeds. From a distance they look like miniature Indian burial mounds from the Midwest.

Benches around the gazebo's perimeter rotted away decades ago. I held Terry's clipboard against my chest. Not sure why I'd picked it up, but I wished I'd thought to bring a couple of folding chairs instead.

Terry wasn't up to sprinting, so he arrived a minute later and wetter. He dug a cigarette pack out of his shirt pocket. Steady drumming rain pelted the shake roof, the flagstone path, the saturated ground—a noise felt as much as heard. The way army ants would sound if they wore steel-toed boots. Terry lit up and inhaled with his eyes closed.

I searched for something to say. But I couldn't commiserate, couldn't offer consolation or empathy. Was he one of the bad guys? He'd sure exploded when Sheriff Marge hinted that he was in on the theft.

I sighed and yanked the stack of papers from the clipboard, then handed it to him. "Here—for your list."

Terry dropped the cigarette butt and smashed it under his toe. "Thanks."

"No problem."

"I mean for helping me when I was out cold. I should've thanked you sooner."

"How do you feel now?"

"Groggy."

"You want me to write while you think? I take pretty good notes."

He handed the clipboard back. "You're going to need more paper."

I filled both sides of Sheriff Marge's notebook page plus the backs of five bill-of-lading sheets while Terry smoked through the rest of his pack. His under-the-table gig with T&T Trucking was pretty regular, with two to three runs per week all over Washington State. If he was telling the truth, the Rittenour delivery would have been his first time crossing state lines.

His hands were still shaking when we finished.

"I think you need to rest," I said. "Come on." I slid my arm through his. "You have an awfully good memory."

"Useful during my forging days." He leaned more heavily against me with each step.

Sheriff Marge was pacing the kitchen, cell phone pressed against her ear. She ran her other hand back and forth through her short hair, making it stand on end. "Uh-huh . . . yeah. Okay."

I marveled at how Sheriff Marge could keep her pants up when there was nothing to hitch her belt above. Her tubular torso extended from shoulders to midthigh. But even under the most strenuous circumstances, Sheriff Marge was always pressed, tucked, and badged in the right places. She hung up.

"Done?" She took the papers and scanned them.

She peered at Terry over her reading glasses. "You've been busy."

He dropped onto a folding chair, but said nothing.

"Here's the deal. I'm not going to arrest you, at least not right now. I am going to call your parole officer, and I'm sure he'd like to talk with you. Since your truck's not going anywhere for the time being and there are no cheap motels around here, there aren't a lot of options. But I can offer you a dry, safe place to sleep. We happen to have an empty jail cell at the moment. We won't lock it. I'm sure the amenities will be familiar. You can have a hot shower, and we'll nuke a frozen dinner for you. I think we have a stash of Lean Cuisines. What do you say?"

Terry picked at his bandage again. "I need a nap."

ooo

I trudged upstairs to my office feeling as exhausted as Terry looked. Probably had something to do with the nerve-racking incidents of the morning. My heart started pounding again whenever I thought about the semi barreling toward Ford astride his tractor. The mental footage was going to plague my dreams for a while. That, and the porta-potty in lumbering flight like an enormous blue chicken.

Lately, Pete Sills had featured in my dreams—for completely different and much more pleasant reasons. He'd pulled me out of a cavern a couple of months ago, but I'd been unconscious at the time and missed out on the tantalizing details. I cringed at the idea that things might become combined in my subconscious soup.

I settled into the padded desk chair and let my gaze wander. The south-facing picture window was alive with wavering streaks of water. Three stories down and thirty yards away, the Columbia flowed high inside bouldered banks, her rolling surface dappled with raindrops. It was probably perfect fishing weather.

Sharp rapping made me swivel around. Rupert leaned a shoulder into the doorframe as though it might fall over without his support, ankles crossed, hands stuffed deep in his pockets.

"Hey, where'd you disappear to?" I asked.

"Got a call from my second-favorite Les Puces dealer." His cap was pulled low over his warm brown eyes. If Rupert were a foot taller and two feet smaller in circumference, he might pass for Sean Connery, until he opens his mouth. He has a deep, gravelly voice, but no brogue.

"Does that mean you booked a flight to Paris?"

"It does."

"And you're leaving me with this—" I waved my arm over the wooden statues.

"Better you than me. And I do hope you enjoy the other statues."

My brow furrowed, then I remembered. "Oh, yeah. Are they just like the *Wind in the Willows* illustrations?" I grinned. Toad, Mole, and Ratty are my favorite talking animals in children's literature.

"So lifelike you'd expect them to invite you along for a picnic."

"Perfect," I murmured. If I placed the characters in a sunny spot, visitors would naturally want to spread their blankets and enjoy boxed lunches in their company.

Rupert chuckled. "You have that scheming look, so I'll leave you to it."

"Call me if you buy anything," I said, but Rupert was already gone. My request was pointless anyway. In his pursuit of oddities and treasures, Rupert forgot all about the less important details, like whether or not the item would fit in a display case.

After pulling my knees up to sit more comfortably cross-legged, I flipped open my laptop. Where to begin? I propped one of the male figures against a stack of books.

"Where'd you come from?"

He gave me the silent treatment, lower lip protruding and ears poised for takeoff.

"I can't post pictures of you on the forums until Sheriff Marge says it's okay, so it looks like I'm on my own."

I sighed. Talking to my dog, Tuppence, at home was one thing. Talking to a wooden statue in my office was quite another. I grabbed a pencil and jotted a list of possible search terms.

"Here we go," I said to my little inanimate audience.

Three hours later, after uncountable rabbit trails, goose chases, and tangents, I'd had my fill of wooden carvings. From whimsical to freakish to downright scary, nothing looked like the statues from the Rittenour shipment.

I balanced my wordless companion across my palm. He was heavy—too heavy for any kind of wood I knew. That could be the key.

I clicked through a few links and found a reference to microscopic wood analysis, where superthin cross and tangential sections are shaved off with a razor blade. The mini chips are examined under a microscope, and the cell structures are compared to known samples for identification.

I dialed Greg Boykin, my graduate-student intern. He'd just returned to Oregon State University with a smaller cast on his fractured ankle. We'd fallen into the same cavern several days apart and had both come out with broken bones. I shifted the sling that held my shoulder in place while my collarbone healed, grateful we'd been rescued. It had been a close call for Greg.

"Hiya. Do you know anyone in the forestry research department?" I asked.

"Uh, no."

"Think you could talk to them anyway? See if someone could do microscopic wood analysis for me?"

"Shoot, Meredith, what are you up to? Wait a minute. I have to write this down."

"Sorry. Are you walking?"

"Yeah. I'm late for class. I still forget crossing campus takes twice as long on crutches." He paused as he rustled through his backpack. "Okay. Ready."

"We had some excitement here this morning. I'll tell you about it when you come up after Thanksgiving. But the net result is that I'm researching wood statues from either Africa or Australia. A comprehensive Internet search came up empty. They're extraordinarily heavy, so I'm hoping the wood type will help narrow the region of origin. If I get approval from Sheriff Marge, I could send one for sampling."

"Sheriff Marge? Was it criminal excitement?"

"Could be."

Greg whistled. "Nothing like a little mystery to get a scientist salivating. I'll find somebody and let you know."

CHAPTER 4

The next morning I hurried to my doctor's appointment. The hospital is in the town of Lupine, the Sockeye County seat and a good half-hour drive east on State Route 14. Besides medical care, Lupine boasts a hardware–household goods–craft supply–drugstore, one diner, a pizza place, a diesel mechanic shop, a post office, and a decrepit library. You can get your needs met in Lupine, but if you want anything fancy—anything designer-labeled, custom-made, or in the luxury goods category—you have to plan an expedition to Portland.

An old Datsun pickup with pale, oxidized blue paint loomed in my rearview mirror. The driver's visor was down against the glare of the rising sun, so I couldn't see his face. I slowed to let him pass, but he dropped back. There was plenty of room and no traffic.

"Make up your mind," I muttered.

A few minutes later, he was on my bumper again. I slowed, and so did he.

"Probably on his cell phone. Good grief."

The Datsun followed me into the hospital parking lot and backed into a slot a few spaces away from where I parked. The driver wore a red baseball cap and sunglasses. He didn't have a passenger. Maybe he was picking somebody up. A makeshift plywood canopy covered the pickup's bed. I smiled at how much I pay attention to pickups now that I own one myself, with a special hitch to tow my fifth-wheel RV. Pretty good for a city-born and -raised girl.

I walked through the automatic sliding doors into the ER entrance and took the first hallway to the left. The X-ray technician leaned against the waiting-room wall, flipping through a *Field & Stream* magazine.

"Hey." He brightened when he saw me. "Maybe today's the day."

"I sure hope so." I followed him into a small white room.

"You know the drill," he said.

I took the sling off and stood with my right shoulder in front of a white box on the wall. The technician strapped a lead apron around my waist and spent a few minutes aligning my collarbone with the film slide. He stepped into his protective cubicle and pressed the button. Then he rearranged me and took one more image.

"You can go wait for the doc. I'll have these ready in a jiffy," he said.

My choices of reading material were the discarded *Field & Stream* and a year-old issue of *Parenting*, so I eyed the water stains on the ceiling. At least the hospital didn't pipe Muzak into its waiting rooms. Hurried rubber-soled shoes squeaked on the waxed floor, accompanied by a clattering gurney. Laughter drifted in from a nurses' station, along with the bitter smell of burned coffee.

"Having trouble sleeping at night?"

I jerked. Had I been dozing? The white-coated doctor stood beside me.

"No. Just been sort of busy."

He grunted and beckoned. I followed him to his cramped, windowless office and slid into an empty chair. He sat on the corner of his desk and gave me the doctor look—the one that feels like they've peeled back your skin and are watching your innards chugging away. I held my breath.

"How's the sling?"

"A nuisance."

"Any pain?"

"Sometimes."

"Show me what you're doing when it hurts."

I demonstrated. "And when I pick up anything too heavy."

"That's all normal. The pain is telling you that you shouldn't have done whatever you just did, so pay attention to it." He handed me a printout. "And do these stretches three times a day to get your range of motion back. No skimping."

I nodded. "So I don't have to wear the sling anymore?"

"Nope. Something tells me you haven't been using it much lately anyway."

"You can tell that from the X-rays?"

He laughed. "Nah. Those motions you just showed me—you can't do those with the sling on."

My face grew warm.

"You have a malunion, which means the broken ends of the clavicle are not perfectly matched up, but it's healing nicely. Most patients get antsy to resume their regular activities, so they fudge with the sling. That's when I know it's time to stop using it. If the break wasn't healing well, you'd still be uncomfortable enough to want the sling."

I exhaled and smiled. "Good news."

"You're free to go. Get some rest."

"Aye aye."

I swung my arms as I walked back to my pickup. The freedom felt good, energizing. Sun broke through the thick overcast cloud layer for a minute—long enough to warm my back.

I hadn't realized how much Terry's parole problems were weighing on me. And the questions about the wooden statues.

My mood lightened as I thought about Pete's invitation to Thanksgiving dinner aboard his tugboat. It wouldn't be too awkward since he'd invited Pastor Mort and Sally Levine and their two teenagers as well.

The spot where the little blue Datsun pickup had parked was empty. I had a lot to be thankful for.

ooo

"Better late than never," I announced as I stepped into the museum gift shop.

"How'd it go—oh, you're sling-free," Lindsay Smith, the cashier and official greeter, said as she rose from behind the counter with a stack of trail maps in her hand. Her face was flushed from bending over, and she pushed her long, blonde hair back into place. "Feel good?"

"Even better than I imagined. Sorry about yesterday."

"No problem. It was nice to have the day off. I went shopping with my mom to get the potatoes, celery, and black olives we still needed for Thanksgiving."

"Have Sheriff Marge or Terry been by?"

"No to Sheriff Marge. Terry's the truck driver, right? I saw the truck parked out there, but I haven't seen him."

I absently spun a postcard carousel rack.

"Somebody else is here to see you, though. A Hamilton"—Lindsay checked a note beside the cash register—"Wexler. He said you knew him. He wasn't interested in looking around the museum while he waited, so I put him in your office."

Black spots appeared before my eyes, and a swirling buzz—the noise of a maddened hive—filled my ears. I forgot to breathe.

"I hope you don't mind. I didn't know what else to do. You've never had a visitor before."

I pressed my hands onto the glass countertop, hoping they'd act as suction cups and somehow hold me upright.

"Are you okay? Did you have blood drawn this morning?" Lindsay placed a warm hand on my cold one.

I waved her off. "Fine. I'm fine." I staggered into the grand ballroom. Right. Left. Right. Left. Breathe in. Out.

He wasn't supposed to be here. That's why I moved to the middle of almost nowhere. To get away from him, the memories, the family pressure. My own quiet spot far, far away. And now he'd invaded it. Why was he always taking what wasn't his?

I climbed the stairs carefully, slowly, like a rickety old man. I needed time to think, put on my polite face, hide the roiling emotions.

I'd thought the confusion, anger, and frustration he'd caused were gone, died out like campfire embers. Oh, no. All it took was the mention of his name and my insides sparked into a wildfire with no warning.

Well, he wouldn't stick around long. He never did. He had the attention span of a fruit fly.

Through the half-open door to my office, I saw his legs. He was sitting in my chair—granted, the only chair in the room—an ankle propped on the opposite knee, the custom-made-loafer-clad foot jiggling *allegrissimo*. Yep, there was only one Ham Wexler.

I took a deep breath and pushed the door open.

The wooden statue he'd been tossing from hand to hand clunked on the hardwood floor. "Oops. Sorry. Wow, you look great." He bent to retrieve the statue. "These things are scary. It would be hard to wake up next to this every morning." He held up the female figure.

The lopsided grin and tiny cleft in his chin that used to weaken my knees seemed immature now in spite of new streaks of venerable gray at his temples.

"That could be an historical artifact."

"Really? How old?" He held the statue at arm's length and peered at it.

I snatched the statue and pressed it against my stomach. "Why are you here?"

"Just wanted to see you. Old times' sake—all that."

I was no longer as young and stupid as I used to be. "No. Not all that. Why?"

"Don't be hard on me. I just wanted to see you. How 'bout some lunch?"

I moved to the side so he had clear access to the door and could leave the more expediently. I also pointed toward the doorway in case the first hint was too subtle.

"Come on, Meredith. Hear me out. I know I was immature, but I've changed. I've certainly changed my mind about you."

"Well, I'm no longer interested in you. That will never change."

"But I'm not talking about dating. I've come to my senses. I'm talking about marriage." Ham tilted toward me, his hand sliding dangerously close to my waist.

I dodged, bumped into a bookcase, and gritted my teeth. "You were talking about marriage last time, too, in case you forgot. With both Sheila and me at the same time." I exhaled. "How is Sheila, by the way?"

"She dumped me right after you did." Ham shook his head and chuckled as though the girl had done something endearing. "You both cleared out on me."

Bitter comebacks blazed around inside my head, but nothing strung itself together coherently. I kept my mouth clamped shut.

"Don't look at me like that. I told you I've changed. I'm up for a judgeship now. It's time I settled down, and you're the perfect woman for me."

I thought my head might blast off, a cranial rocket.

I could bash his head in with the heavy statue. Death by ugly blunt object. Let the punishment fit the crime, tra la.

Ham kept talking, but all I heard was *wah—wah—wah*. He amped up the Pepsodent smile, turned on the charismatic charm that wooed juries, especially if they were predominantly women, and did what he did best—schmoozing.

Had he said *judgeship*? That would be the day.

Oh, judges were elected, weren't they? Which meant he had to fool only the voting public. Unfortunately, he could probably do so with his hands tied behind his back. He had a top-notch glib-o-tron. I wondered if he'd dyed the gray streaks in order to appear more trustworthy.

"I can tell you're distracted," he rushed on. The man never drew breath. "I probably interrupted your work. You know what—I'll come back later, when you're feeling better. We can talk over the details. Arlene will be thrilled."

I hated that he called his mother by her first name. Wait, what was Arlene going to be thrilled about?

"Catch you tomorrow, sweetie." Ham winked, spun on his heel, and left.

"No!" I shouted, but it came out like a death groan.

I hadn't nodded my head, had I? Given him any kind of encouragement? I was certain I hadn't agreed to anything.

"Aaargh!" I slammed the statue on the desk, then froze, realizing what I'd done.

CHAPTER 5

The thing was indestructible, or was it? No chunks broke off. I gingerly tipped the statue to standing and felt its weight shift. Something rattled inside.

I lifted the statue, and a circular wooden plug fell out of the bottom. A dull gold-colored rod, six or seven inches long and the thickness of two fingers, thudded on the desk. The statue was suddenly as light as balsa wood, an empty shell. I sat down hard.

Then I jumped up, shut the door quickly, and locked it. My mind raced. This was a whole new ball game.

In a way it explained a lot. If the statues were just a foil, a transportation mechanism, then they wouldn't have documentation or historical record. Maybe they'd been carved in the past few months, which would account for their poor workmanship. But importing gold wasn't illegal, was it?

I flew to the computer and checked the US Customs list of banned items. No, gold was okay. Of course, the government would appreciate anyone importing gold to declare that fact. But there were no limits. Unless.

Unless the gold was from a short list of countries or a much longer list of "specially designated nationals"—in other words, terrorists, warlords, and their power brokers and financiers.

I blew out a big breath. What had we stumbled into? Did Terry know? Was he really good at faking bumblingness? Because a scheme like this seemed way over his head.

Maybe it wasn't gold.

I rummaged through the file cabinet's bottom drawer and found a digital scale. I switched it to metric and balanced the metal rod in the scale's plastic bowl. One kilogram exactly. The weight of a standard gold bar. And the density seemed right for gold—the heaviness for its relatively small size.

The rod didn't have any markings. I'd never seen a gold bar in person, but online pictures showed they usually had their source, weight, and purity—and sometimes a company name—stamped on the surface. The rod appeared to have been molded to fit in the statue's hollow core. The sender had probably wanted to remove any chance of tracking the gold based on its markings. But it was ready to remold into a new bar.

It might not be pure.

But if it was . . . I found the price of gold. While it fluctuated, $1,500 per ounce was a reasonable average. I scribbled on a notepad, converting metric to American weights, then multiplying. If the missing thirteen crates had a similar number of statues each, and there was a kilo of gold in each statue, the value of the shipment came close to $6 million. No wonder someone had lain in wait for it.

My stomach burbled, reminding me that I'd missed lunch. But I felt more nauseated than hungry and was as shaky as Terry without his nicotine.

Steady on. I examined each statue, pried out the plugs, and lined up seven more gold rods beside the first one.

My eyes flitted over the bookshelves lining the walls, the file cabinet, the stacks of research papers. There was no place to hide the gold rods, no place to secrete something so valuable, not even in the rest of the museum. The original safe in the basement would be a joke to a professional safecracker, probably even to a thug with a sledgehammer.

I wrinkled my nose. Why was my first instinct to hide them? They should be exposed. The criminals—I had no doubt of that now—needed to be found, their motives uncovered.

I dialed Sheriff Marge and burst into explanation when she answered.

"Slow down," Sheriff Marge said in a low tone. Someone shouted obscenities in the background.

"Where are you?" I asked.

"At the Randalls' place. You probably don't know them. He takes her hostage every once in a while, usually around the holidays. Family tradition."

"Oh." Suddenly my problem didn't seem so urgent.

"I'm going to have to think about this one," Sheriff Marge said. "And figure out which federal agency to contact. They're all closed for Thanksgiving anyway. The bank in Lupine's probably closed, too. Find a good place to hide them and don't tell anyone else for now."

Rapid popping—*tat tat tatatatat*—sounded, then a thud and Sheriff Marge breathing hard—whooshing like she was running.

"Are you okay?" I yelled.

"Yeah. I gotta go. He's actually firing this time." The line went dead.

I slumped, pressed my hands over my face, and offered up a prayer for Sheriff Marge's safety, and for Dale's and the other two deputies'. With such a small department, they were probably all on the scene or would be soon.

I thought about calling Sandy, Dale's wife, but maybe she didn't know yet. And knowing might be worse. I shook my head. I'd wait. The sheriff and her deputies dealt with this kind of stuff all the time.

I stretched my fingers and watched them shake. My insides were a zinging bundle of nerves, all because of eight gold rods and gunfire on the phone. Oh, and Ham. His proximity was the nagging dread I'd been feeling. My stomach clenched and considered vomiting. Nope—empty. I needed food, but first I had to hide the gold.

Where?

Where, where, where?

Certainly not in plain sight. The museum's security system was lousy. The rods had to go someplace unexpected. But where?

The freezer in the staff kitchen? A toilet tank? An air vent? A linen closet?

I went back to the toilet-tank idea. The chamber pot exhibit was in one of the family bedrooms and had an attached private bath. To prevent leaks, the water had been turned off, so the tank should be dry. The mansion had fourteen private baths in addition to the public restrooms on the main floor. Even if potential thieves hit on the idea of a toilet tank, they'd have a lot of places to check.

I stuffed the rods in a messenger bag I kept on hand, cracked the door open, and peeked into the hallway. The museum had closed an hour ago, so all visitors and Lindsay should be gone. With the bag slung over my good shoulder, I tiptoed down one flight of stairs to the chamber pot room. The wooden floor creaked with each step, the noise echoing off the walls and high ceiling. So much for stealth.

The bathroom door squealed like a disgruntled baby pig as I pushed it open. It locks only from the inside, so we never lock it—but we keep the door closed to discourage unsanctioned exploration by visitors.

Rust powder lined the bone-dry toilet tank and stuck to my skin as I set the rods one by one in the bottom. I replaced the lid, then used my sleeve to wipe my dirty handprints off the white ceramic. Anyone who saw me now would know I'd done more than research today, but the museum was dirty enough that I could probably brush off their questions by saying I'd been working on a display. Which could be true, depending on how you looked at it.

While washing my hands in the main restroom, I thought about the statues. If I left them out, anyone would be able to see they'd been tampered with and know the contents had been removed. They had to be hidden, too. Somewhere else. But where?

Ahh. The place every kid would know and every adult would forget. I hurried upstairs.

Wedging the plugs back into the bottom of each statue wasn't as easy as I'd expected. More of a mind puzzle to match up jagged edges and smooth bumps. I kept one plug for research purposes and packed the statues into the messenger bag.

In a hallway in the servants' quarters, I opened a hinged wall panel and suspended the bag from a knob inside a dark cavity.

The knobs are both a curse and a blessing. Rupert's great-great-uncle planned on having a large family when he built the mansion. He thought of everything, including an escape route should a child happen to tumble into the laundry chute. Two sides of the chute are like an early version of a rock-climbing wall, studded with knobs and toeholds. The housekeeping records are peppered with staff complaints about clothing and linens hanging up on the way down. I felt a rush of gratitude for the ancestral Hagg's foresight.

Food. My stomach could no longer be ignored. And I needed ingredients for tomorrow's feast.

I dashed off a short note and stuffed it along with the wooden plug into a padded envelope. No harm in a little inquiry—Sheriff Marge had other things to worry about. I collected my purse and walked through the empty museum. The place was becoming quite a keeper of secrets.

The phone rang as I pulled the seat belt across my lap—and reveled in how much easier that was to do without the sling.

"Hey, Meredith," Greg said. "The forestry department—well, pretty much the whole school—has cleared out for Thanksgiving. I found one graduate teaching assistant who thought they could do microscopic wood analysis, but she told me to check back after break. Sorry."

"No problem. Sorry to make you run around. I'm sending you a wood sample anyway. Maybe next week they'll be able to look at it. What are you doing for Thanksgiving?"

"Getting together with a couple friends from Thailand. We've never cooked a turkey before, so we're going to give it a shot."

"Remember to remove the neck and gizzard from inside."

"The what?"

"You don't have to eat them. Just take them out. They're usually wedged pretty far into the cavity. And keep an eye out for a gravy packet, too. You'll see what I mean."

Greg laughed. "You're making me nervous. Is your date with Pete still on?"

"It's not a date. There'll be a boatload of people, literally."

"Tell yourself that if you want—but the rest of us, we know what's really going on." Greg hung up before I could argue further.

Huh. It was *not* a date. It was one of those nice things people did to make sure singles weren't alone for the holidays. That's all. Really. Pete had invited me, but Sally Levine must have suggested it to him. He'd had to ask because we were gathering on his boat. No big deal.

My stomach rumbled like a freight train, reminding me of more pressing matters.

ooo

I parked next to a flashy red Corvette in Junction General's lot. The sports car was so new it still had a temporary license taped in the rear window. It definitely did not belong to a local resident, since the trunk wasn't big enough for hauling firewood, fertilizer, or even an economy pack of toilet paper. I opened my truck door carefully, not wanting to give the shiny paint its first ding.

Junction General carries about a million products two deep. Gloria Munoz, the proprietress, does an amazing job of keeping the small town of Platts Landing supplied with essentials. Thanksgiving—when everyone wants to buy a lot of the same few items—is a little trickier. I hoped Gloria had stocked up on cranberry jelly and stuffing mix.

I grabbed a plastic shopping basket and wandered down the canned-goods aisle. Gloria knelt on the worn black-and-white checkerboard floor, refilling the cream-of-mushroom soup spot on the bottom shelf.

She looked up and smiled. "Selling like hotcakes. Can't stand the stuff myself."

"Me neither. I was assigned a vegetable dish, but I think I'll make some kind of salad and skip the green-bean casserole altogether."

"Good call. Hey, I met your friend Hamilton Wexler."

I almost dropped the basket.

"I just finished fixing up the studio apartment upstairs, and he's my first renter. He reserved it for a week, for the holiday. Said he was in town to visit you. He sure seems like a nice guy."

I hadn't even known there was an apartment above the store. My mouth hung open. Gloria was fishing for gossip. She settled on her haunches, waiting for a juicy detail.

But my brain still hadn't kicked into gear. Why did Ham make me speechless? When I got angry at anyone else, my vocabulary exploded, but even the mention of his name had a horrible, stifling effect on me.

"Uh," I said.

"And you're having Thanksgiving dinner with Pete Sills." Gloria's eyebrows arched.

Of course she knew—everyone knew. Good grief. I was single-handedly providing soap-opera programming for the whole town. And it wasn't even my fault.

Metal bells clanked against the glass door as someone barged inside.

"Gloria," a voice called—Ham's voice. "The lightbulb over the dining table just burned out." He came around the end of the aisle and halted.

"Meredith! But of course we'd bump into each other, wouldn't we—in a town this size. You're buying food. How about dinner? I'm just whipping up a little stir-fry upstairs. Chop. Chop." He aimed his fingers like pistols and jerked them, gunslinger style.

I had no idea what that had to do with chopping.

"What do you say?"

"No," I grunted.

"Aw, come on. I'm a great cook. When we're married, I'll cook for you all the time, whatever you want."

Gloria knocked over several soup cans, and one kept rolling—*woowr, woowr* down the aisle.

"Married? I—"

I was cut off by the metal bells clanking violently, like someone whacking a wind chime with a baseball bat.

A petite blonde stormed past the end of the aisle, skidded, and turned back. A blur of flying pink and yellow and sparkles—glitter eye shadow, dangly earrings, and rhinestones on flip-flop straps. She was wearing flip-flops in November? And fuchsia toenail polish.

"You bastard! Do you think you can hide from me?" Miss Glitz screamed. Her hand closed around a can of chili. "Did you think I wouldn't find you? Your little midlife crisis in the parking lot was a dead giveaway. How dare you!"

"Now, Val, I told you I needed a break. There's no need to get excited." Ham's voice skipped up an octave.

Val slung the can sidearm and nearly clocked Ham, except he dodged at the last nanosecond. He seemed familiar with this kind of target practice.

The can sailed past my shoulder, and I hit the floor beside Gloria, sending a painful jolt through my ribs and collarbone.

The next can plowed into a shelf above us, shattering a pickle jar.

Gloria's brown eyes widened, and she started to rise. "Hey! Watch it! You can't—"

I grabbed her and pulled her back down. A box of spaghetti broke overhead, and pasta sticks rained on us.

I felt for my phone in my jeans pocket, then realized I'd left it in the truck.

"My store—" Gloria moaned. "Thanksgiving. What'll I do?"

I squeezed her arm. "Go the other way, toward the back. Scootch on your stomach." I gave Gloria a shove to get her going. "Lock yourself in your office and call Sheriff Marge. Go!"

Gloria army-crawled down the littered aisle, through tomato sauce and mustard—the colors of the USC Trojans. I always think the players look like picnic condiment sets when they take the field. I shook my head. Focus, I needed to focus.

When Gloria seemed safely out of reach, I followed, dragging the shopping basket with me. Val and Ham continued their shouting match, but my mind raced through options for putting a stop to it, safely.

Apparently Ham's smooth, lawyerly manner didn't mollify some people. Val certainly had grit—she was no pushover. But she was also a really good pitcher, and somebody was going to get hurt. I had to catch Val from behind—that arm was a deadly weapon.

At the end of the aisle, I crawled to the next row—the beer and soda-pop aisle—and trotted to the front. I took a quick peek and saw Val's skinny bottom stick out past the potato-chip display as she bent to pick up another missile.

"I even grew out my hair for you," the girl screamed.

I had a feeling Val was beyond being pacified by diplomacy and negotiation. I glanced at the shopping basket in my hand—too light and clumsy to throw accurately. Instead, I plunked it on my head like a helmet and charged.

I meant to round the corner, tackle Val in a tight embrace, and take her down, but a slick of something—Alfredo sauce?—turned the linoleum into a skating rink. I streaked past, behind an oblivious Val, and smacked into the sturdy, buffalo-plaid-jacketed Pete Sills, who'd just stepped through the front door. He caught me and kept me from a headlong slide into the checkout counter.

A wild pitch—orange marmalade—took out a row of cereal boxes on the top shelf and splattered at our feet.

Pete dragged me outside and removed my headgear.

"Do those people need help?" he asked.

I felt my cheek. Grid marks from the shopping basket were imprinted in my skin from my collision with Pete. I was also sticky. "I don't know. Maybe it's better to let them have at it. I'm sure Ham deserves whatever he gets, and he can pay for the damage."

"Ham?"

"Hamilton Wexler—my ex-fiancé." I gulped, but it was too late to take the last part back. I hadn't discussed much of my past with Pete, particularly not any previous romantic attachments. "We're not—absolutely no way—" I shook my head. The right words wouldn't come. "Never."

"Okay." Pete pulled me against his chest.

I pressed my nose into the scratchy wool of his jacket and inhaled the scent of licorice and dusty wheat.

"You want to tell me about the shopping basket?" Pete's low voice rumbled in my ear.

I scrunched up my face, glad he couldn't see. How mortifying. "I watch a lot of football. I needed protection," I mumbled. "It seemed like a good idea at the time."

Pete's muscles quivered ever so slightly. He cleared his throat.

Gravel sprayed in all directions as the sheriff's Ford Explorer skidded into the parking lot.

Sheriff Marge popped out of the vehicle like a pinched watermelon seed. "What's going on?"

I reluctantly pulled away from Pete. "A couple's fight. From what I could gather, he jilted her, and she doesn't appreciate it."

Sheriff Marge moved toward the store.

"Watch out—she has a great throwing arm," I called.

Sheriff Marge kicked the door open and bellowed, "This is the sheriff. Hands where I can see them. Now!"

I moved to follow, but Pete held me back.

"Just give her a few minutes to do her job." He wrapped his arms around me and rested his chin on top of my head. "Besides, you're still shivering."

I closed my eyes and leaned into him. Were we actually cuddling? There might have been cuddling a couple of months ago when he'd carried me out of the cavern, but I'd been unconscious and missed out on how good it felt. Since then we'd seen each other when he was in town, talked some, but never touched—not even a handshake. Maybe I needed to throw myself at him more often. It seemed to produce good results.

"Ready?" Pete said.

"Huh?" I snapped out of my reverie.

"I don't hear any more yelling inside. But I did hear your stomach growl."

CHAPTER 6

Ham and Val sat on the floor, propped against opposite ends of the checkout counter with their hands behind their backs. Ham had the beginnings of a doozy of a shiner, and his face was already swollen around a small gash on his cheekbone. Mascara streaked Val's cheeks, and her hair was disheveled. One flip-flop was missing.

Ham opened his mouth to speak, but I glared at him. For once it worked—he stared at the floor.

I almost smiled, then darted a quick look back at Val. I'd been tempted to throw things at Ham a time or two (or three) myself. And Val had done it. I admired her spirit, but she looked crushed at the moment.

Gloria, shaky but standing, arms clenched across her abdomen, nodded as Sheriff Marge gently asked questions and scribbled in her notebook. Gloria was a living Jackson Pollock painting—discordant red and yellow smeared her turquoise shirt and khaki pants. I looked down to find I could pass for Gloria's twin. I noticed for the first time that I reeked of dill-pickle juice.

Pete placed a few dollars on the counter and led me to the hot-foods display. He grabbed two shriveled corn dogs off the rotisserie and handed one to me. I held it dumbly.

"Eat."

I nibbled.

"You hate corn dogs, don't you?"

I nodded.

He squirted mustard on a paper tray. "Have some. It helps."

"I'm wearing enough to slather a hundred corn dogs."

"This is clean." He thrust the tray toward me, and I dipped.

"Mmm." I dipped again.

"What'd I tell you?"

But all I could think about was that I was double-dipping with Pete.

Sheriff Marge joined us. "All right. Fill me in." She looked haggard, more wrinkled than yesterday. Her gray eyes were tired. But she held her stubby fingers poised, ready to take notes.

I kept it short and left out the part about my attempted tackle. I figured Sheriff Marge wanted to know only what Val and Ham had done.

"You know Val"—Sheriff Marge checked her notes—"Valerie Brown?"

"Never seen her before. I'm a little surprised. She doesn't seem like Ham's type."

"Which is?"

"Uh—classier?" I glanced at Pete, but his deadpan face didn't offer any encouragement. "I mean—well, it's just that Ham's a lawyer, and he's sort of picky about his image. He usually dates women who enhance his reputation."

"I understand he dated you."

"Yeah, but that was before—and anyway, I dumped him."

"Uh-huh."

"He was two-timing, three-timing—I don't know how many of us he had going. I got out as fast as I could when I figured that out."

"Know why he's here?"

"He stopped by the museum today and talked for a while. Honestly, I didn't listen very much—you know, with everything else that's been going on."

"Did you know he was coming to see you?"

"No. And I really wish he hadn't."

Sheriff Marge pushed up her Stratton hat brim and tucked the notebook back into her chest pocket. "Okay. That's enough for now."

"What about the incident at the Randalls'?" I asked.

Sheriff Marge exhaled. "My deputies are wrapping up the scene."

"What does that mean?"

"It means, fortunately, we didn't have to shoot him. In the end he did it himself."

I wanted to fling my arms around Sheriff Marge and squeeze. No wonder she seemed zapped of her usual vitality. She must live with a load of heartache for the people she protects. But she's not the type of woman you hug.

"And his wife?"

"Hysterical. But she'll get over it. Doesn't take long to figure out life is better when you're not married to a man like that." Sheriff Marge rubbed her forehead. "Back to the matter at hand, I'm arresting Ms. Brown for assault and battery and destruction of property. Mr. Wexler is free to go and seek medical attention if he wants. I had to cuff them both since I'm dealing with this incident by myself and couldn't trust them to leave each other alone." She sighed. "I hate domestic disturbances."

"Would you like to come for Thanksgiving dinner?" Pete asked.

My heart swelled at his thoughtfulness, although I thought his timing could have been a little better. Sheriff Marge is a widow, and her grown sons are scattered across the country—too far away to come for weekend holidays.

"That's kind of you. But I think I'll be doing paperwork tomorrow." Sheriff Marge shrugged and turned toward her prisoner.

ooo

The next day Tuppence and I strolled around the campground while the yams baked. I assumed Pete's oven would be full, so I wanted to have all my assigned dishes ready to serve when I arrived. And it didn't hurt to get in a little exercise before the big meal.

Dark clouds hung low, their bottoms dropping away in filmy mist layers. I shivered and hunched into my coat. Usually thick clouds offered protection from extreme temperatures, but it was bitingly cold. The weather was about to change, for the worse.

Tuppence felt it, too. She sniffed with her nose high in the air and stuck close to my leg.

I caught a whiff of smoke—campfire smoke. A thin plume rose above the Russian olive grove where the unimproved tent sites are. Tenting in winter in the Columbia Gorge meant the camper was either a diehard with all the necessary equipment or dangerously ignorant.

I strode through the wet grass with Tuppence on my heels. Spots of pale blue and old lumber appeared between the olive trees' low branches. I squinted and sped up.

"Halloo," I called before pushing through the brush into the clearing. I didn't want to startle the occupant.

He leaped out of his lawn chair anyway and crouched slightly. His right hand slid inside the open front of his down vest, his lips pressed into a tight line.

I held out my empty hands instinctively. My heart thumped fast. The driver of the Datsun pickup who'd tailgated me on the way to the hospital. Was it coincidence to encounter him twice in as many days?

"Sorry to startle you. There just aren't that many campers here in November, so I thought I'd say hi."

The man glared at me, but slowly straightened.

"I'm Meredith and I live here year-round." I was about to introduce Tuppence when I noticed she'd made a circle around the campsite and stretched in from behind the man to sniff his pant leg. I shifted my gaze quickly back to the man's face. He seemed the type who might give an inquisitive dog a swift kick. "Are you visiting friends or family in the area?"

"Looking for work," the man grunted. "Wind farm."

"Oh, yeah. I've heard it's hard work—lots of climbing towers while hauling heavy parts." Probably not the most intelligent remark, but it was too late to retreat. I could play a ditzy female if I needed to. He didn't have a tent set up. "Do you have a way to heat that?" I pointed to the plywood canopy over the pickup's bed.

"I'll be fine." He scratched his chest and pulled his hand back out of his vest. He looked like any other laborer—plaid shirt under the vest, jeans, boots. The baseball cap shadowed his face. I could tell only that he was swarthy, with dark eyes like holes and a small nose—what you'd call a button nose on a kid, but it wasn't cute on this guy.

Tuppence moved on to inspect the Datsun's rear tires. The man didn't seem to have any camping equipment other than the lawn chair—unless he hadn't unpacked yet.

"Good luck with your job search." I forced a cheery smile.

He shrugged.

"Well, it's nice to meet you. What's your name?"

"Ferris."

First name or last name? I didn't dare ask. "Happy Thanksgiving."

I hightailed out of the clearing, willing Tuppence to come without being called. The hound caught up to me within a few yards.

"Does he make you nervous, too?" I asked in a low voice.

Tuppence snorted.

I knelt outside my RV and tousled Tuppence's ears. "Want to come to Thanksgiving dinner with me? I don't think Pete'll mind. Anyway, he'd better not."

ooo

Tuppence and I walked down the slippery dock to Pete's tug. It was tied in one of the wide berths at the Port of Platts Landing and exhibited the only signs of life in the vicinity. Golden light from its windows reflected on the wet planks. Everything else was a shade of gray in the early dusk created by the overhanging cloud layer.

Pete opened the door, took my heavy basket, and held my hand as I stepped over the high threshold. Tuppence clambered after me and followed her nose directly to Pastor Mort Levine's ankles. He bent to scratch the dog's back.

"I hope it's okay that I brought Tuppence," I said.

"She's as welcome as you are." Pete's crinkle-cornered blue eyes just about did me in.

Sally Levine greeted me with a quick hug. "Smells delicious. What'd you bring?"

"Yams, salad, pecan pie." I sniffed appreciatively. "I was going to say the same, though. Have you been cooking all afternoon?"

In unison, Sally said, "No," and Mort said, "Yes."

"Well, it doesn't feel like it," Sally explained. "Pete did the big stuff—the turkey, stuffing, and mashed potatoes."

"Where are your kids?" I asked, looking around.

"The youth group had a chance to help feed the homeless in Portland today," Mort said. "They were excited to go, and it'll be a good experience for them."

"You ready to answer their questions when they get back?"

"I'm old enough to know I don't have all the answers." Mort chuckled. "And I think my kids have figured that out, too."

I settled on a built-in bench across the table from Mort and watched Pete and Sally work around each other in the tiny galley. The appliances and fixtures were strictly utilitarian and compact, but it also looked as though Pete had everything he needed. It was a couple of steps up from a typical bachelor pad. Probably on par with my trailer, if I wanted to be honest. And cozy.

"Where's your crew, Pete?" I asked.

"Carlos and Al hitched a ride with a cousin to their mom's place in Twin Falls. Bert's sister lives in Vancouver, so I dropped him off there Tuesday night."

"You can run the tug with only three?"

"We didn't have a load, so yeah. Both Carlos and Al can man the engine room. We're pushing a barge of earthmoving equipment up to Boardman this weekend, so the guys'll all be back onboard early tomorrow."

"What's the craziest cargo you've ever hauled?" Mort asked.

Pete laughed. "Probably the four hundred head of bison a Montana rancher was moving to eastern Oregon. They had them loaded in pens on the barge, but the pens were too big, which allowed the weight to shift too much. I white-knuckled the whole trip. It was my first live animal load. Now I insist on approving the holding pen size and placement before we leave the dock, regardless of whose barge it is." He shook his head. "I can't afford to lose a load, even if it was someone else's mistake."

"You must meet all kinds of interesting people," Sally said.

"Oh, yeah—mostly real nice folks, but there've been a couple nut cases, too. I still worry about the guy who bought the parts to make three wind turbines. Had a chat with him when I delivered them—he said he wanted to live off the grid, but he also spent quite a lot of time ranting against the government. Those things'll produce way more power than you need for a household or farm—definitely overkill for one guy and his family. I talked to the local US Marshal's office just to make sure he was on somebody's radar. They said they were already keeping an eye on him."

"If you had one of those turbines, you could probably run a massive year-round marijuana grow without anyone noticing—if your power use is off the grid," I said. "Wow. Think how much harm a person could do if they had their own large energy source."

"I still feel bad," Pete said, "about reporting him to the authorities."

"Sounds like you did the right thing," Mort said. "You had good reason to be concerned."

We crammed together in the dining nook, bumping elbows as we passed mountains of food and heaped our plates.

"This is worth praying over," Mort said as he squeezed Sally's hand. "Lord, again, as always, Your grace abounds. Let us never forget to seek You first, above all else. Thank You for this excellent company. Amen."

I love Mort's relaxed and honest prayers, as though he's talking with a good friend—the kind of friend who's comfortable with silences.

I ate slowly and listened to the conversation eddy and bubble with laughter. Pete's shoulder pressed into mine. I glanced at his chronic three-day stubble. He'd be kind of scratchy to kiss. Maybe I wouldn't mind.

"Did you hear about the excitement at Junction General yesterday?" Sally asked.

My stomach plunged. The thought of Ham ruined my appetite.

Pete's warm hand rested on my knee. My fork slipped and clattered on my plate.

"A domestic disturbance," he said. "A couple of out-of-towners."

"What a pity," Sally replied. "I heard there was quite a mess." She looked at Mort. "The store was closed today. Do you think—?"

"Yes," Mort said. "Let's go in the morning and see if Gloria needs help."

"Who's ready for dessert?" Pete asked. He rose to fetch the pies.

I exhaled. Considering how fast both truth and rumor spread through Platts Landing, I was grateful word of the semitruck robbery hadn't made it to Mort and Sally. I didn't feel prepared to fend off questions about the stolen goods and what might or might not have been inside the crates—or inside a toilet tank in the museum.

Mort checked his watch. "I always have time for dessert. But I'm a little worried about the storm coming in tonight. I hope the kids get home ahead of it."

"Storm?" I asked.

"They're predicting freezing rain, or sleet—what is the proper term? And high winds." Sally handed me a plate with slivers of pecan, apple, and pumpkin pies on it. "Figured you'd want a sampler."

"You got that right." I grinned.

"Sleet falls in pellet form, sort of like hail," Pete said. "Freezing rain is liquid that freezes on contact, and it's the worst. Working the tug is treacherous in freezing rain. I hope it clears by morning." He nudged me and pointed at the huge slice of pie on his plate. "Pecan is my all-time favorite."

"Really? Well, there's plenty more where that came from." I flushed. That might have come out the wrong way. When I caught Sally giving Mort a little sidelong smile, I knew for sure. Uh-oh. Good thing Pete's mouth was full, or he might have compounded my embarrassment.

"You know, sweetie, I hate to rush, but maybe we should head home," Mort said, "so we're there when the kids arrive."

Sally patted his shoulder. "I'll just pack up some of this food for Pete."

I stayed on my bench, out of the way, since the galley was already a tight squeeze with three moving bodies. Sally heaped leftovers into containers and stacked dishes in the small sink.

"I'll help clean up," I called, "so you two can get going. Thanks so much for all the yummy food."

"You make sure to take some of this home, too, Meredith," Sally said in her kindergarten teacher voice.

Mort helped Sally into her coat and hoisted their cooler. "Weighs as much as when we came."

"Oh, it does not." Sally gave him a playful smack. "Night, all."

A blast of frigid air from the open door raised goose bumps on my arms. I scooted out of my seat and stood next to Pete to wave good-bye to the Levines. I shivered, and he put an arm around me.

"Boy, I bet the temperature's dropped ten degrees in the last couple hours," he said.

We stepped back, and he closed the door. "You should leave soon, too. There are extra bunks since the crew's not onboard, but, uh—well, it wouldn't—"

"No. Of course not," I said. "This town already has enough to talk about."

I hurried to the sink and turned on the tap. "I did want to take a couple plates to the jail. I feel sorry for Val—being locked up on Thanksgiving, and a Lean Cuisine frozen dinner just can't compare to a real home-cooked meal."

I wanted a plate for Terry, too, but didn't want to open that subject with Pete. "Sheriff Marge or a deputy are bound to be around as well, so I thought I'd take extra." I looked at Pete over my shoulder. "If you don't mind?" I plunged my hands into the hot, soapy water.

"Sally left enough to feed an army." Pete came up behind me and placed a hand on my shoulder. He spoke quietly. "I don't mean to sound like I'm kicking you out, but I want you to leave right away. The roads are going to be slippery, and since you're driving to Lupine and back—can you call me when you get home? I need to know you're safe."

I turned to him, hands dripping, and studied his face. His sapphire-blue eyes were serious. He handed me a dish towel.

"Actually, how about if I come with you?" he said.

What could I say? He'd want to know who Terry was, and I might spill the beans about the gold in the statues. So many bits of research information were swirling around in my head, I was afraid something might pop out at the wrong time. I hated not being able to tell him.

I glanced down, but Pete was standing so close, all I could see was his shirt front. I was suddenly very warm. "I—I was kind of hoping to have a conversation with Val, um—you know—I just—" I took a deep breath. "I know how hard it is when you find out someone you trusted isn't trustworthy, and I thought maybe she'd need to talk about it. I don't know if she'll want to see me, but I thought I'd try."

Pete tipped my chin up. The crinkle-corners were back. "Then let's get you on the road."

We quickly filled plates and wrapped them.

Pete went first, carrying my basket and truck keys. I followed, gripping the ramp railing with my bare hand as a smattering of rain flew at a forty-five-degree angle. I patted my coat pocket. No lump. My gloves were on the top shelf of the closet at home. Tuppence trotted, head down and ears flapping, straight for the open truck door and jumped onto the seat. Pete hurried around to the driver's side and helped me in.

"Call me when you get home, no matter how late it is," he said as a wind gust flipped up his coat collar. "You can always spend the night at the jail if you need to."

"Very funny."

"I'm serious." He shut my door.

CHAPTER 7

On the open highway, gusts buffeted the truck, but very little rain dotted the windshield. I gripped the steering wheel and pressed on the accelerator. The Columbia River Gorge is like a funnel for the large basin east of the Cascades. Cold air rushing through the channel brings several severe storms each winter. Exciting and potentially dangerous.

I was worried about talking to Val. I'd been so angry at Ham's duplicity when I'd first discovered it that I'd fled. His mother, Arlene, had helped me pack. She was the only one who'd supported my decision, who'd understood. My mother and stepfather had told me it wasn't a big deal, that these things happen and I should just learn to live with them. At least Arlene admitted to her son's faults, even as she fervently hoped he'd outgrow them.

But Val had seemed desperate to hang on to Ham. Maybe if she knew what he really was, she wouldn't feel so betrayed. I jerked the steering wheel against a blast of wind. Poor kid. It was worth a try.

I figured Sheriff Marge would forgive me if I sped a little, and I raced into Lupine twenty-five minutes later. It felt deserted. Even the tavern parking lots were empty. Yellow light emanated from most houses' kitchen windows, and blue glows shone from the living-room windows—televised football games in full swing.

I pulled into the courthouse parking lot next to a deputy's cruiser and rolled my window down half an inch, giving Tuppence a tiny crack for fresh air.

I pushed the intercom buzzer on the secure side door used as the jail entrance and smiled up at the video camera.

Deputy Archie Lanphier's scratchy voice came over the speaker. "Hey, Meredith. Is that a picnic basket?"

"Yep."

"Then I guess I'll let you in."

The lock clicked, and I pulled open the door. In the dingy sloped hallway, the air grew cooler and mustier with each step downward. The jail was in the basement, and it stank of moldy carpet and fresh paint. I waved at the second camera, and the next door clicked open.

Archie pulled his feet off the desk, stood, and hitched up his gun belt and pants in one motion. "To what do I owe this pleasure?"

"I was hoping to visit your prisoners—well, your prisoner and your guest. I brought them some home cooking." I set the basket on the desk and lifted out the loaded plates. "I have an extra plate for you, too. I'm sorry you drew dungeon duty today."

"It's not so bad. We're splitting half shifts. Dale took the morning stint, and Owen Hobart covered this afternoon. So I've already had my big meal and caught the end of the Steelers game." He inspected a plate. "These dill potato rolls look like they have Sally Levine's fingerprints on them."

"Wow, you're good."

Archie laughed. "Naw, I recognize them from the Sunday potlucks, and I make sure to grab a couple every time I see them. I'm a meat-and-potatoes-and-bread kind of guy." He pursed his lips. "Okay if I save this for later?"

"It's all yours. How are things in there?" I tipped my head toward the steel door to the cells.

"Quiet. That little gal can get fired up, but I think she's worn herself out now. Sort of don't know what to do with her except give her tissues. She's kind of weepy." Archie looked uncomfortable and hitched up his pants again. "They're talking about letting her out, so that'd be good."

"Out?"

"Yeah. Gloria doesn't want to press charges and neither does the fellow she hit with the can. Sheriff's been working on the prosecutor's office to drop it with maybe some restitution fees or something. Gloria just wants her to promise she'll never go inside Junction General again."

I laughed. "I can understand that."

"Say, I heard you know the guy—what's his name? Some meat. Anyway, that you're, uh, friends—from way back."

"Not exactly. How's Terry?"

"Quiet, too. Calls his mom a couple times a day. Seems nice enough, keeps to himself. I'd go crazy if it was me—I'd never voluntarily spend time in jail. Course, he's not locked in."

I pointed to the plates. "Can I take these in to them?"

"You didn't hide knives in the cranberry sauce or anything?" Archie laughed at his joke but stopped when he saw my scowl. "Sure. I just need to wand you." He looked uncomfortable again.

I pulled my keys out of my pocket and tossed them in the picnic basket. I held my arms out while Archie rapidly waved the metal-detector wand along my limbs. I tried to keep from smiling. Archie is downright fidgety around women.

"I'll buzz you through."

Plates in hand, I pushed the door open with my behind. Terry was in the closest cell in the row of six concrete-block cubicles. His barred sliding door was open, and he sat on a folding chair with his feet propped on the lower bunk. He was reading a John Grisham novel.

"Learning anything?" I asked.

"Nope." Terry stood quickly and tossed the book on the bed.

I handed him a plate. "We crammed as much as we could on one plate, so hot and cold foods are mixed together. Sorry I can't microwave it for you."

"For me? Looks great." He peeled back the plastic wrap and inhaled, holding the plate just inches under his nose. "Wanna sit down?" He gestured toward the folding chair.

"I'm going to deliver this plate to the other inmate, but I'll stop by on my way out."

"Yeah . . . Val." Terry nodded. He lowered his voice to a hoarse whisper. "I'm worried about her. I think that good-for-nothin' broke her heart."

I raised my eyebrows. Terry—the relationship counselor?

"I've been trying to cheer her up, but that ain't exactly my strong suit." He scratched the back of his head with his free hand.

"Hey, your bandage is gone."

"Nick came and checked it. Said the cut's healing okay. Itches like h—crazy."

I grinned and walked toward the makeshift curtain strung across the aisle before the last cell. Women's quarters.

"Val?" I called. "Okay if I come in?" I poked my head around the edge of the fabric.

"Yeah," she said, barely above a whisper.

Val sat curled on the bottom bunk with her feet tucked under her. Her face was blotchy and devoid of makeup, hair pulled back in a long ponytail. Still in the pink designer sweat suit, but no longer sparkly.

"I brought you Thanksgiving dinner." Val's cell door was closed and locked, so I pushed the plate into the rectangular food-tray slot.

Val slowly unwound her legs and shuffled over. "Thanks," she sniffed.

"You probably don't know me—I'm Meredith."

"Yeah, I know." Val stood with her arms limp at her sides, her head hanging as she gazed at the floor. "You're the one Ham really loves."

I snorted. "Ham doesn't really love anyone except himself. I found that out the same way you did, a couple years ago."

"But he came back for you. He wants you. He said you'd make the perfect judge's wife."

I spluttered. There just weren't words.

I stamped my foot hard on the concrete floor, then winced when the pain registered. "Aaargh! That man is so self-absorbed he doesn't hear no when it's shouted in his face."

Val looked up, startled. "You mean he does that to you, too?" She returned to the bunk and sat on the edge. "Oh." She stared at her feet and wiggled her toes inside jail-issued slipper socks. "I thought he wasn't paying attention." A little smile slid across her face. "So I threw things for emphasis."

I giggle-snorted.

Val giggled.

"You might be the only woman Ham's dated brave enough to actually give him what he deserves," I said.

"Oh, no. He deserves way worse."

I sat cross-legged on the cold floor and leaned toward the bars. "So what is this about a judgeship?"

Val came over and sat facing me. She laced her fingers through the bars. "He's running against Anita Hadley for a Superior Court seat."

"Anita Hadley? Ham dated her when they were both in the prosecutor's office. She hates his guts."

"Exactly. The campaign's getting nasty. Ham figured having a respectable soon-to-be-wife by his side would help dispel some of Anita's allegations. My family's too blue-collar, so I'm not qualified for the position."

"You wanted the position?"

Val shook her head. "I don't know what I was thinking. I just hate the backhanded way it all happened." She sighed. "Campaigning isn't really my thing, anyway. I want to be an executive assistant during the day and play with my dog in the evening. That's enough excitement for me."

I nodded. Yep, a good job and a dog—all a girl really needed. "What allegations?"

Val's eyebrows arched. "You'd think Anita lives under a slimy rock with all the things she's suggested—bribery, general fiscal irresponsibility, philandering, cronyism—just because she's not the one getting the favors." Val picked at her nail polish. "She's nasty, but I wonder if some of her claims are true. Ham just breezes over it. He won't explain, at least not to me."

I wrinkled my nose. I didn't want to tell Val that I wouldn't be surprised if some of the allegations were true. My experience with Ham was that he danced along the edge of morality and every once in a while tripped over the line.

I heaved a sigh. Maybe Val had made a narrow escape, the way I had. "Well, if you're still here this weekend—which I hope you're not—but if you are, I'll bring my dog in. She's really good at letting people pet her."

Val smiled. "Thanks. It was awfully nice of you to bring food." She stood and brushed off the seat of her pants. "Awfully nice to come at all."

I smiled back.

Terry was scraping the last of the gravy from his plate when I returned.

"How's your mom?"

"Fretting." Terry shook his head.

"You can go home, can't you?"

"Yeah. Probably just get a slap on the wrist for parole violation. But I'm staying."

"Why?"

Terry spread his arms. "Best alibi around."

"What do you mean?"

"I'm no dummy. There's something going on with the stolen shipment. Sheriff keeps asking me questions." He ran a finger inside his shirt collar. "Something big—and I don't know nothin' about it. I don't wanna get blamed for something I didn't do."

I opened my mouth, then closed it. I couldn't agree or disagree. What did he know about the shipment? Maybe more than he was so adamantly denying.

"Thanks for dinner. Best I've had since Mom's goulash."

I nodded and rapped on the door for Archie to let me out.

ooo

I nearly did the splits on the sidewalk. An invisible ice glaze covered everything. The rain was coming faster now, adding layer upon layer. I slid my feet slowly, heading for the grass and bark dust in the dormant flower beds, where the surface was rougher and safer.

I pounded on the truck's door handle to break the ice shield. Tuppence whined as I scooted into the seat.

"I know, old girl. I shouldn't have stayed so long."

I'd had studded tires put on the truck a few weeks back, but the ice was probably thicker than the stud depth. I let the truck roll straight back out of the parking spot. Now was not a great time to put a dent in Archie's cruiser.

We crept through town—which didn't bother anyone because no one else was out. Locals know better than to drive in these conditions. On the highway I was glad to see that the few other cars on the road were moving as slowly as I was. No impatient tailgaters tonight.

The pickup slid a few times, and the windshield coated over even with the wipers going full speed. I pulled onto the gravel shoulder, stepped out of the truck, and inched around the hood to scrape the ice off. My hands were painfully stiff, and I rubbed them until I could grip the steering wheel again.

Shoulders scrunched into tight knots, I leaned forward, peering into the dark. The headlight beams lit up the slanting rain—the drops looked like a rapid meteor shower through the black night. Ice chunks clicked and crackled as they slid around on the truck's surface and broke free.

At last I pulled into the Riverview RV Ranch's drive. As I followed the circular road through the campground, I strained to see the blue Datsun pickup in the tent area, but it was too dark to tell if Ferris was still there. I nosed my truck close to the fifth-wheel's overhang.

"Whew." I kneaded my neck muscles. "Come on, Tupp. Be careful when you jump."

I grabbed the side mirror to keep my balance. Tuppence scrabbled on the pavement, legs splayed. We skated to the steps. I beat on the door with my fist to loosen the ice and finally pried it open. The door snapped shut behind us like an air lock. The ice coating muffled sounds and insulated the trailer into a cozy cocoon.

I slid my arms out of my dripping coat and tossed it in the bottom of the shower. The alarm clock in the bedroom flashed—the power had already gone out at least once. I snagged a bath towel and rubbed Tuppence down.

I checked the time on my phone—10:38 p.m. Awfully late, but Pete had insisted. I dialed.

He picked up on the first ring. "Where are you?"

"Home."

He exhaled.

"I'm fine. Sorry to make you worry. How are things on the tug?"

"Dogged down."

"What?"

"The watertight door clamps are called dogs. *Dogged down* means I'm floating safe and dry."

I sighed and massaged the back of my neck with my free hand. After a few seconds, I realized I should probably say something. "When will you be back in town—after the run to Boardman?"

"A week, probably."

"Want to come for dinner then?"

"Yes."

I pictured him leaning against the galley counter, broad shoulders stretching his buffalo plaid jacket, and those deep-blue eyes. Mmm.

"Meredith?"

"Hmm?"

"Are you falling asleep?"

I yawned. "Just dreaming, but that's a good idea. 'Night."

ooo

I awoke in a cold sweat—miserably damp and chilly. I groaned and reached for the comforter. My hand splatted on saturated fabric—frigid, saturated fabric. I sat up and clicked on the light, except the light didn't click on. Groaning louder, I thrashed the covers off my legs and rolled out of bed. The carpet squished beneath my feet and instantly froze my toes.

"No," I moaned. "No, no, no, no, no."

I rummaged through drawers in the dark until I found a flashlight. Shivering, I directed the weak beam around the room and caught something twinkling on the ceiling. A line of dangling droplets stretched from one side of the room to the other. While I watched, half of them shimmied free and were replaced by new, growing drops. The whole roof seam must have popped open.

I squeezed my eyes shut. This kind of thing didn't happen in real houses. Living in a fifth-wheel didn't feel so glamorous right now—not so free-spirited and fun.

I gave myself a mental kick in the seat. *Quit that. I love where I live and how I live. It's a fact of life that bad weather wreaks havoc on RVs. What's a leak once in a while?* I pushed straggly curls out of my face and clenched my teeth to keep them from chattering.

Okay, so my problem was more like Niagara Falls. Everything was soaked—pajamas, blankets, pillows, mattress, carpet. The vinyl wallpaper at both ends of the ceiling seam bulged to about halfway down the wall. A grand mess—a freezing-cold grand mess.

It looked as though the dresser and closet were safe for now. I stripped and threw my pajamas in the shower, then pulled on a sweat suit and two pairs of socks. I hopped around on the bathroom linoleum, trying to warm up.

"Brrr, brrr, brrr." Not good enough. I stumbled down the steps to the kitchen.

No power meant no furnace heat. Maybe the gas fireplace would still work, since it ran off the propane tank. I scuffed into the living room and tripped over Tuppence's big pillow bed, plunging to a soft crash landing on the sofa. The dog groaned and stretched.

I fumbled for the switch and found it, and blue flames flickered behind the glass screen. I hugged my knees to my chest and stared into the fire. Tuppence nudged my foot and whined softly.

I rubbed her ears. "Sorry for the intrusion. My bed's all wet." I wrinkled my nose. "You don't snuggle as well as Pete does, but I'll let you on the furniture for one night." I patted the sofa cushion, and Tuppence clambered up beside me.

I pulled her warm, furry weight across my lap and scratched her belly. "You're a good dog," I murmured. "Better than a blanket."

Tuppence shifted awkwardly, and her cold nose found a gap between my sweatshirt and pants.

"Yow! Not that. Keep your nose to yourself."

Tuppence yawned.

I settled back, working my fingers through her silky fur. I realized how much I liked Val's honesty about missing her dog. There was no reason why two women who'd dated the same man couldn't be friends, was there? Especially if they agreed the man was a cad.

When it was light, I'd figure out whom to call. Maybe I should have spent the night on the tug, dogged down and warm. Pete was protective of my reputation, though, and thoughtful—a vast improvement over Ham's callousness. I couldn't stomach the idea of what rumors would have flown if I *had* spent the night.

Nevertheless, I wished Pete were here.

CHAPTER 8

I waited until the semi-decent hour of eight a.m., then called Mac MacDougal, owner of the Sidetrack Tavern and cabinetmaker for the museum. Along with Sheriff Marge, Mac knew nearly every person in the county—at least every beer-drinking, football-watching male. I figured the best person to fix my leaky roof would also have those three traits.

I stood in the bedroom doorway surveying the damage and explained.

"Jim Carter," Mac said. "Best handyman around."

I wrote down the number. "Thanks, Mac."

"Hey, do you need a place to stay? You could stay here. No strings or anything—I mean unless you want, but, uh, well, yeah—you could have my bed." My mouth fell open. "I have an old army cot to sleep on," Mac added quickly.

I inhaled. "Um, thanks, but my sofa's pretty comfortable. I'm fine."

"Well, my offer stands if you ever need it."

"Right."

"Hey, can you stop by sometime? I want to show you a new display-case design I'm working on."

"Um, sure. In the next couple days?"

"Sounds good. Tell Jim he gets a free drink from me for helping you out."

I hung up without replying. I didn't know whether to laugh or be irritated. Poor Mac. He needed a girlfriend—but some other girl. Val was newly available. Hmm.

I dialed Jim Carter's number.

"Jim's Rental Center."

I described my predicament. "Do you think you can fix my roof?"

"Maybe."

"Uh, could you come out to look at it, or should I tow the trailer to you?"

Jim sighed noisily into the receiver. "I guess I could come out."

"Great. When is good for you?"

Jim shuffled through papers and muttered. I held my breath, fearing he would say his next opening was in two weeks. "I can probably get there in half an hour."

I almost dropped the phone. "Oh, thanks. Spot C-17."

"Hafta rearrange my deliveries," Jim grumbled, and hung up.

I wrinkled my nose and stared at the phone. What a crab. Half an hour. I tossed the phone on top of the dresser, grabbed an armload of clothes, and dashed for the shower, grateful the power was back on and the rain had stopped.

I rushed through an abbreviated morning routine and started a full pot of coffee, hoping the aroma would make Jim more amiable.

Metal clanked outside, then thuds shook the trailer. I poked my head out the door. Overall-clad legs stood on the top rung of a stepladder. The man's top half rested on the fifth-wheel's roof.

"Hello," I called.

A horrible ripping sound stopped my greeting, and a strip of flashing sailed over my head. I ducked.

The ladder wobbled, and I grabbed it. Jim grunted and pushed himself farther onto the roof. More ripping and crunching—a wood-splintering sound.

"What are you doing?" I yelled.

Jim scooted to the edge, found the top of the ladder with his foot, and peered down. The skin under his brown eyes drooped in wrinkles, reminding me of a bloodhound. "Grab the blue tarp from my truck. And bungee cords."

I scowled. But since I know nothing about RV repair, I decided to follow orders. And prayed Jim knew what he was doing.

Jim's white utility pickup and small trailer blocked my drive. Two porta-potties in the trailer made the connection in my mind—the same Jim that Ford had said would not be happy about picking up the damaged porta-potty at the museum. No wonder he was crabby. I found the tarp and bungee cords behind the passenger seat and handed them up to Jim.

"Not the cords." He tossed them back down.

Jim wrestled with the tarp, flipping the edges off the front and both sides of the fifth-wheel's high section. He clomped down the ladder and hooked bungee cords through the tarp's grommets and attached them underneath the overhang. He emerged, huffing, and set his fists on his hips.

"What I thought. Water leaked under the seal and lifted it when it froze last night. Gotta dry before I can fix it."

Jim was an Eeyore-faced man, narrow at the forehead and jowly about the chin. A yellow Caterpillar baseball hat rested on prominent ears.

"But you can fix it?" I asked.

"That's what I said."

"I want to apologize for the porta-potty accident at the Imogene a few days ago. I'm the museum curator."

Jim grunted.

"Would you like some coffee? It was kind of you to come so early." Jim patted his overall bib in the vicinity of his stomach. "All right."

He followed me into the trailer and sat heavily on a dining chair. Tuppence ambled over to inspect. He stroked the dog's head.

I set a steaming mug in front of him. "Milk? Sugar?"

Jim waved his hand and slurped the scalding liquid.

"Bagel with cream cheese?"

"Yeah. Okay."

I popped a split bagel in the toaster, leaned against the counter, and tried to think of something to say that wouldn't offend him. "Mac MacDougal recommended you."

More slurping.

"He said you're the best handyman around. You must have tons of experience. What are your specialties?"

"This 'n' that. Appliance repair, remodeling, excavating, hauling—got the latrine servicing business on the side, and U-Haul rentals."

"Excavating?" I perked up. "We have several large statues that need to be installed on the museum's grounds. Would you be interested?" I realized I hadn't even seen the *Wind in the Willows* statues yet—they were still impounded in Terry's damaged semitrailer. I hoped the crates and packing material had protected them during the truck's slide and near-collision.

"Ground's saturated. I'll take a look."

"I'd really appreciate that." I slid a plate onto the table.

Jim crammed a huge bite of bagel in his mouth. He stood and stomped up the steps to my bedroom. I cringed and tried to remember if there was anything personal lying about.

"Carpet's gotta come out."

I followed him up the stairs.

Jim was already kneeling in a corner, pulling the carpet off the tack strips. He jerked a large section up, creating a miniature tidal wave toward the stairs.

"Hang on—hang on." I dashed for the kitchen and my roasting pan. I shoved the pan under the lip of the top step. "Okay. Ready." I wadded towels around the pan.

Jim had the carpet and pad out and rolled up in his pickup's bed in fifteen minutes. He hauled in two heavy-duty fans and set them in the corners of the bedroom.

"Be back in a couple days," he shouted over the din. "What color?" He pointed to the floor.

Everything in the RV is a shade of brown with wood stain. A mechanical engineer's idea of decorating, meant to hide wear and tear from road travel. "Uh, a neutral? Tan, beige—something like that."

Jim scooped up the remains of the bagel and left, letting the door bang.

I shook my head. Not the friendliest fellow, but I couldn't complain about his response time. What a mess.

I dragged a bath towel across the kitchen floor to mop up the water trail left by the soggy carpet. Tuppence nosed around and got in the way.

"Should we live in a regular place, Tupp? Would you like that better? We could live in Gloria's new apartment once Ham's gone."

The dog did a full-body shake, her long ears slapping under her chin and over her head.

I waited until she finished. "Are you sure?"

Tuppence snorted.

"I guess we both need our freedom, huh?"

ooo

When I arrived at the museum, Lindsay flagged me down with a sheaf of papers. "Could you look over my application? And write a reference for me?"

I veered into the gift shop. "So you're ready?"

"As ready as I'll ever be, I guess." Lindsay sighed. "If a college application is this hard, what are classes going to be like?"

"It feels like a test, doesn't it?" I laughed. "But you're going to do just fine. I know it."

Lindsay flipped her blonde hair behind her shoulder. "I'm hoping to finalize the essay this weekend and submit the whole thing on Monday. The reference needs to arrive by December 1."

"No problem. Who are your other references?"

"Greg said he'd write one, and I thought I'd ask Sheriff Marge."

"Having the county sheriff as a reference will look good."

"I hope she writes more than 'Haven't had to arrest her yet.'"

I chuckled. "Nah, your letters are going to be effusively positive. I'll give you a copy of mine." I climbed the stairs.

I stopped in midstride at my office door, pivoted, and tiptoed back down one flight of stairs to the chamber pot display room. Looking quickly in both directions, I entered and nudged the door closed behind me. I slipped into the bathroom, peeked in the toilet tank, counted, and breathed a sigh of relief.

I'd forgotten to ask Lindsay if there were any visitors in the museum. Anxious that one or several might appear at any moment, I hurried back to my third-floor sanctuary and slid into the lumpy, leather-covered chair. Whew.

It took a while for my heartbeat to stop pounding in my ears. The sooner the gold was someplace safe, the better. But Sheriff Marge had a lot going on, so I decided to give her some time before I called to nag her—like maybe ten minutes.

I spread out the pages of Lindsay's application. It was surprisingly well done. Lindsay is a little ditzy sometimes, but she'd put a lot of thought into her answers. *Good job, kiddo.* I grinned. After all my careful prodding, it was satisfying to see Lindsay develop a goal and really go after it. The fledgling was going to leave the nest, provided she was accepted at Washington State.

I typed an honest letter extolling Lindsay's virtues. I mentioned reliability, work ethic, and unflagging cheerfulness. And the fact that Lindsay was a football encyclopedia with a knack for explaining the game to the uninitiated in clear and simple terms. In other words, she'd make a great sports broadcaster or coach. Plus she was cheerleader cute, but I didn't step outside politically correct bounds in my note. The sports-management program chair would find that out when Lindsay went for preview weekend.

I skimmed for typos, then hit print. The ancient printer started its ten-minute warm-up exercises. Maybe Rupert would buy me a new printer if I put it on my Christmas list. But if I had to decide between a new printer and whatever Rupert was scrounging at the Les Puces flea market, I'd take the flea market find any day.

Someone rapped on the doorframe.

I spun around. "Hi. I was just thinking about you."

Sheriff Marge skirted a filing cabinet and leaned against a bookshelf, arms folded across her midsection. I thought she might be offended if I offered her the only chair in the room—the one I was sitting on—so I stayed put.

"How was your Thanksgiving?" I asked.

"Hectic. Archie told me you stopped by the jail and brought food for everyone. Thanks for doing that."

"Glad to. So is Val getting released?"

"Yep. Already done—first thing this morning." Sheriff Marge shook her head. "When you have two domestics in one day—one ending in a suicide and the other involving a repentant hurler of soup cans—well, then your perspective changes. Your friend Ham had a chat with the PA—one prosecuting attorney to another—and they agreed."

"He's not my friend. What about damages?"

"He's paying for everything. Even spent yesterday helping Gloria clean up. That sure smoothed things over."

"He is smooth." I pressed my lips together.

"Uh-huh." Sheriff Marge sighed. "Now, about our other situation." She reached out and pushed the door shut. "Got calls back from a couple of interested agencies this morning. Treasury and the FBI. They don't agree with each other about whose domain this problem might fall under. They're both sending an agent, but with the holiday and their incredibly heavy workloads"—Sheriff Marge sniffed—"it'll be a day or two before they get here."

I raised my eyebrows.

"Uh-huh. Have you tried contacting the gallery the crate was addressed to?"

"No. Was I supposed to?"

Sheriff Marge shrugged. "No, but I'm curious."

I pulled over my copies of Terry's bills of lading and picked up my cell phone.

Sheriff Marge tapped my arm. "Use the museum line. Let's keep it a call from one art institution to another."

I found the Rittenour Gallery's phone number on Terry's paperwork and dialed. I hit the speaker button, and we both listened to the buzzing tone.

A woman answered after the sixth ring. "Crosley & Associates. How may I help you?"

"Uh-oh," I said. "I thought I was calling the Rittenour Gallery."

"No gallery. Just a bunch of bean counters." The woman laughed. "The office is closed for the holiday, but I have a ton of stuff to catch up on, so here I am. Answered the phone out of habit. We get lots of calls for an aquarium-supply company. I guess they had our number before we did. We do have a Rittenour here—Earl Rittenour—one of the CPAs, but no gallery. What number did you dial?"

I took a breath—because the woman didn't seem to—and read the phone number off the bill of lading.

"That's our number, all right. I bet you want to talk to Earl. He collects art—if you can call it that. Horrible little wood carvings from

Africa. They're just grotesque, but he seems to like them. I wonder if he's thinking of starting a gallery? I bet Mona doesn't know. She's the bossiest, clingiest wife I've ever met. That's probably why he had you call here. Just a minute—I think—" The woman's voice faded. Then she was back. "Here it is. He's on vacation for a few days, and I don't want to give you his home phone number just in case he's hiding something from Mona—that would be terrible, wouldn't it? So here's his cell phone number. Ready, hon?"

I gulped and grabbed a pen. "Yep."

I scribbled Earl's personal number on the bill of lading. "Thanks so much."

"Anytime. You have a great day. And remember Crosley & Associates for all your accounting needs."

Sheriff Marge and I enjoyed a few moments of silence.

"Whew," Sheriff Marge finally said. "If only it was always so easy."

"Call his cell phone?" I asked.

"Might as well. Let's hope Mona doesn't answer."

No one answered.

After the generic voice-mail instructions and beep, I said, "Uh, hi. This is Meredith Morehouse from the Imogene Museum in Platts Landing, Washington. There was a little mix-up in a delivery on Wednesday, and we ended up with a crate addressed to you—or, uh, to the Rittenour Gallery, I guess. Anyway, the secretary at your office gave me this number. I was wondering if you'd like to make arrangements—" I lifted my eyebrows at Sheriff Marge, who circled her finger in the air. Keep going, keep going. "Uh—to pick up the crate, or let me know what you want done with it. Thanks." I recited the museum's phone number and hung up.

"Sheesh. Trying to tell the truth, but not the whole truth, is hard." I exhaled. "Did I sound too phony?"

"Good enough. We'll see what happens."

"What about the, uh—the contents of the crate?"

"You have them squirreled away?"

"Yeah."

"Then let's leave them where they are for now. I'm sure the feds will have an opinion about what to do. In the meantime, the fewer people who know about them, the better."

CHAPTER 9

After Sheriff Marge left, I began a landscape plan for the children's garden. I wanted it placed on the sloping lawn between the museum and the river, where the view was spectacular. Several large shade trees dotting the area would give picnickers options.

I cut out five small bits of paper, labeled them "Mole," "Ratty," "Toad," "Badger," and "Otter," and pushed them into different configurations. Having an odd number was good, but who should go in the middle? Toad, of course. Or maybe placing them in a circle would be better. But wouldn't they all want to see the river? A semicircle. Aha. It would be so fun to add props—a rowboat with a luncheon basket tucked under the seat, a horse and cart, an old jalopy for the motorcar—but I was getting carried away.

Maybe it'd be better to forgo formal landscaping and instead encourage native wildflowers to fill in around the statues—camas lilies, lupine, pink phlox, yellow arrowleaf balsamroot, asters. I made a list. Someone from the Washington Native Plant Society could give me more ideas.

"Do you always work so hard?"

I closed my eyes and concentrated on breathing. Ham. I should have told Lindsay to bar him from the museum, but it hadn't occurred to me that he would return.

"I just wanted to apologize for that little misunderstanding the other night." Ham sat on the edge of my desk and reached for my hand.

I tucked my hands into my lap, under the desk, and frowned at him. His right eye was surrounded by a deep-purple shadow.

He looked around. "Hey, you got rid of those horrible wood statues. I'm glad. Those things gave me the willies."

My eyes widened—I had to change the subject, fast. "I heard you convinced the PA to drop the charges against Val, and you helped Gloria clean up the store. That was nice of you. Thanks."

Ham shrugged. "Least I could do. It was partly my fault. I should have been clearer about my plans with Val."

"Uh-huh."

He leaned toward me. "About my plans to propose to you. You will, won't you? Marry me? You know we're great together." He slid closer.

I pushed with my foot, and my chair rolled back, bumping to a stop against a box of Native American stone fishing weights. "No."

I almost cheered. I'd said it! Clearly, distinctly, and unequivocally. Ham no longer held me tongue-tied.

"Meredith, I know my record's not flawless. I've made mistakes. But I'm going to show you that I've changed. I'm a new man, compassionate and sensitive."

"You're running for office."

"Yes!" Ham's crooked grin widened. "Fundraising, banquets, press conferences—we'll make a great team. And once I'm on the bench, I'll be invited to lecture at law schools, and you can go with me. Your background in the management of a cultural institution will be very impressive. Maybe they'd let you lecture, too—for arts programs or something."

"You pretty much have to reach the Supreme Court level before anyone's interested in listening to lectures."

Ham waved dismissively. "I'll get there."

"You've got to be kidding."

"No. I'm the right age to start this process. Experienced and mature, but still early in my career. I have a real shot at it."

I snorted.

A look of consternation crossed Ham's face, and he opened his mouth. The ringing phone cut off whatever he'd been about to say.

I scooted my chair to the desk and answered. "Hello?"

"Jim Carter's here," Lindsay said. "And he wants to know where you want the holes." There was a scratchy sound, and then Lindsay asked in a muffled voice, "What's that mean?"

"He's going to install the new statues—outside."

"Oh, good. The way he said it, I thought he brought a wrecking ball and was ready to start swinging it."

"I'll be right there."

God bless Jim Carter and his impeccable timing.

I stood. "The answer's no. It will always be no. I realize this is difficult for you to comprehend, but I can assure you I will never change my mind. Go away—shoo." I made flapping motions toward the door.

Ham flushed. Little beads of sweat popped out on his temples. "You need to hear me out."

"No." I wheeled and strode out of my office, leaving Ham and his thick skull behind.

Jim stood in the gift-shop entrance, hands stuffed in his pockets, elbows protruding and feet spread wide. I peered around him, at Lindsay, who shrugged an "I didn't know what to do with him" motion, palms up.

"Let's go outside." I tucked a hand inside his elbow and led him along the muddy footprint trail he'd deposited on his way in.

A small, rusty dump truck pulling a trailer with an even smaller, rustier backhoe on it sprawled lengthwise across several parking spots, blocking in Ham's shiny red Corvette.

"Oh. First thing—you need to move your truck so that car can leave," I said.

Put a dent or two in it for my sake, I thought, but held my tongue.

Jim moved his truck and rejoined me on the lawn, shovel in hand. We strolled toward an Oregon white oak. Since it wasn't crowded by other trees, the branches arched in a perfect dome close to sixty feet across.

"I don't want the digging to interfere with any root systems, so can the statues go on the south edge of this tree? In a semicircle, facing the river?"

Jim checked the oak's canopy, took fifty paces out from the drip line, and stabbed his shovel in the ground. "Tree's not full height yet. Here?"

I moved beside him and looked out over the river. Sunlight found a few gaps in the clouds and sparkled on the choppy gray surface. Rolling green velvet hills flanked the Oregon side, dwarfing a mile-long train that looked like a toy chugging east on tracks just above the waterline. "Perfect."

Jim pulled a couple of flag markers out of his bib pocket and poked the wires into the ground. "I'll dig a semicircle, then lay a good foundation before placing the statues. Gonna make a mess of the grass, but I'll reseed."

I nodded. "Okay."

"Statues?"

"In the semitrailer." I pointed.

Jim started walking, and I trotted to catch up.

The trailer's sides rippled and bulged in spots, as though the cargo had been sloshed back and forth. Chunks of the open rear door hung from the roll-up mechanism—the thieves' handiwork exacerbated by the near-collision.

Jim climbed in and sized up a crate. He tried to lift a corner, grunting, but couldn't budge it.

"Don't have a loading dock, do you?"

"At the museum? No. It was built in 1902 as a private residence, so no loading dock."

Jim lifted his hat, scratched, and resettled it. "We'll need Verle's tow truck."

"You sure?"

Jim heaved a sigh.

"Right. Okay. Should I unpack the statues so they're not as heavy?"

"Nope. Don't want to break them. Easier to put straps around the crates."

"When can you start?"

"Now." He squatted at the edge of the trailer and swung his feet to the ground.

I fell into step beside him on the trek across the parking lot.

"My wife left me a few years ago," Jim said.

My breath caught, but I kept looking straight ahead. Did he want me to say something? What?

"I guess I'm not that exciting. She always wanted to go do stuff, and there's not much to do around here. You seem like the type who's content to stay home."

I am the type who prefers to stay home. One of the many reasons Ham's offer was so unappealing. But should I admit it? What was Jim driving at? My stomach twinged nervously.

"I, uh—I was wondering." Jim took off his hat and scratched again. "Uh, sometimes I drive up in the hills to pump latrines at wind-farm construction sites. It's a real pretty drive. Maybe, uh, you'd like to go with me sometime."

Shoot. It probably was a gorgeous drive. Shoot. "Uh," I said. "Can I think about it? The museum keeps me pretty busy."

"Yep." Jim put his hat back on. "Let me know. I go out regular."

We'd reached his dump truck and trailer. He unhooked the chains securing the backhoe, clanked down the ramps, and climbed into the backhoe's cab. The engine rattled to life, coughing gritty black smoke out the exhaust pipe. Jim looked over his shoulder and started inching the machine backward. I decided it was time to get out of the way.

I replayed our conversation while trudging upstairs to my office. Should I have done something differently, said something else? Had I led him on? I'd met him only that morning. Of course, he'd already been in my bedroom. Good grief.

I'm always surprised by these displays of male interest. Am I missing clues somewhere along the way, or do they truly come out of the blue? It could be that the men are just lonely—really lonely. Jim was right about there not being much to do out here—unless you're a die-hard fan of hunting, fishing, hiking, or windsurfing. And even those have seasons—times of year when prudence or the law dictates abstinence.

I settled into my chair, happy to be alone with my thoughts—happy to be alone at all. Ham was gone—his car hadn't been in the parking lot when Jim and I returned from examining the statue crates. I soon became absorbed in documenting items.

Rupert, at the board of directors' behest, has been scouting for years to build up a museum-worthy collection. His tastes are a little eccentric, but the museum now has a native animal taxidermy collection, a sizable group of Victorian ball gowns with accessories, a farming-implements display, an exhibit of chamber pots through history, and a meager assortment of Native American artifacts. There are tons more items that have not yet been documented or grouped into coherent displays—that's my job. I've managed, in my two years as curator, to photograph maybe 20 percent of the undocumented items.

I opened a folder of digital photos—a series of unmarked Limoges snuffboxes—and assigned ID numbers and typed descriptions into the record. I sighed. There was so much to research. If I put the boxes on display now, their placards would read, "Limoges snuffbox. Date unknown. Manufacturer unknown." I could write a display description about their general history, manufacturing techniques, and what other purposes the little boxes were used for, but that was it.

Maybe someday—if I catalog faster than Rupert buys—I'll catch up with him. I shook my head and grinned. Rupert was my godsend—giving me a job when I most needed one. And, on top of that, giving me a job I love more than I ever dreamed. When I left my hectic management position at Nike, I had no idea what museum curators did or that it was even a legitimate occupation.

And Ham wanted me to go back—back to the insane world where people who claimed to be your friends competed with you, climbed over you, in pursuit of more prestigious jobs and more impressive stuff. Or more prestigious and impressive spouses, as the case may be. Yuck.

Nope. Never, never, never again. I'd stay right here in Platts Landing, where I got asked out by the porta-potty man.

Speaking of which—I hurried to the window. The lawn past the white oak had been scalped. A neat semicircular trench had been dug in the middle of the scarred area.

It reminded me of the last deep hole I'd seen—at the family cemetery on Julian's ranch, for his son, Bard. I frowned. I should go check on Julian, see how he was holding up.

Jim was hosing off the backhoe bucket.

I shut down the laptop, grabbed my coat and purse, and dashed downstairs.

"See you later." I waved when Lindsay turned from restocking the custom-printed coffee mugs in the gift shop.

I picked careful steps across the shredded lawn and met Jim halfway as he wound up the hose.

"Wow, you're fast."

He shrugged. "This slope has good drainage. Gravel'll be here in the morning."

"Gravel?"

"To keep the statues from settling. We'll pour the concrete bases on top of the gravel."

"Oh. Right. So you work Saturdays?"

"I work when there's work to do."

"Well, thanks. I'm pretty excited about these statues. It'll be great to see them in place."

"What are they?"

"The statues? They're characters from the children's book *The Wind in the Willows*. There should be a rat, a mole, a toad, a badger, and an otter."

Jim's eyebrows pulled together. "Rodents."

"But they're cute, and they talk. Well, at least in the book they do."

"Huh. Learn something new every day."

"So I'll see you in the morning?"

"Yep. Seven thirty."

I wrinkled my nose. I didn't want to miss the excitement of a gravel truck, but seven thirty a.m. on a Saturday? Oh, well, I'd probably be awake anyway since I'd be sleeping on a couch in the same room as a snoring dog.

I drove to Mac's Sidetrack Tavern, a brick-red building—a box, really, with antennas and satellite dishes all over the flat roof. Mac had a healthy business—mainly because he guaranteed that every NFL and college football game could be seen on one of his big screens.

Friday night and the parking lot was half-full. In another hour it would be packed, and dirty pickups raised on knobby tires would be parked along the edges of the road outside the entrance as well. I figured I'd better hurry so I wouldn't take Mac away from his duties at his peak time.

I tucked my purse under my arm, skirted a couple of puddles in the gravel parking lot, and pulled open the heavy wooden door. Blinking while my eyes adjusted to the dim interior, I strolled toward the bar. Mac, knit cap on his head and towel flung over his shoulder, was slicing something behind the counter.

I leaned over to peek and sniffed appreciatively—lemons.

"Hi, Meredith. Arnold Palmer?" Mac asked.

"Hi, Missus Morehouse," Ford called loudly.

Several men straddled stools along the bar, but I spotted Ford at the far end. He grinned and sucked on a straw in a Dr Pepper can. I waved, then squinted. Next to Ford sat Ferris, the driver of the blue Datsun pickup whom I'd seen at the hospital and in the campground. He nodded curtly. I gave a tight smile and turned to Mac.

"Nothing for me, thanks. I just came to see your new display-case prototype, but it looks like you're busy already. Have you talked to that man sitting next to Ford?"

"A little. I can spare a few minutes. You want to come back to the shop?"

"You sure?"

"Yep." Mac signaled a waitress to come take his place and lifted the hinged counter for me to pass through. "Jim taking care of your leak problem?"

"Yeah. Thanks."

Mac led me into a back room piled high with kegs and boxes, then down a short corridor to the rear exit. A few steps across an alley stood Mac's pole barn workshop. He lived in the loft and tinkered with woodworking tools on the main floor in his spare time.

When Mac opened the door, the scent of sawdust and sweet pitch surged into the cold air. He flipped on a bank of light switches, and the large open room flickered into view. I saw the case immediately.

"Oh, wow. It's beautiful." A clear acrylic box topped a rectangular base covered in a highly polished burl veneer.

Mac grinned. "Thought you'd like it. And look at this."

He opened a panel in the base and pulled a handle hidden inside. The wooden floor of the acrylic box dropped out of sight.

"What's that for?"

"In case you have a particularly valuable item you don't want in public view for some reason, you can lower it into the base. I haven't figured out the electronics yet, but I think this could be rigged with a timer to secure the item when the museum closes."

"I don't think we have anything that valuable," I said. "But then again, I never know what Rupert's going to send."

"Ford was talking about some statues you just got—African or something, and really heavy. He said they're scary ugly, which means they're valuable, right?" Mac laughed.

My stomach dropped. Ford had been talking about the statues? I hadn't thought to warn him not to—I'd forgotten he'd helped take them to my office. Oh boy.

Mac was still talking. "I could install little spotlights to highlight the items inside, too. That way you can put the case anywhere and not have to worry about whether or not the overhead lighting is good enough."

"Terrific," I murmured.

Mac looked at me quizzically.

"I love it," I said, louder. "Really love it. Rupert's scavenging at the Paris flea market, so I'll let you know if he finds something that would be right for this case."

I moved toward the door, then spun back. "Actually, I could use three right now. I can't believe I didn't think of it sooner. I just documented Limoges snuffboxes today, and they'd be perfect in cases like this." I placed my hand on the case and peered into the open bottom. "Yeah. How long will it take you to make two more?"

Mac whistled and exhaled. "Maybe a month? They're pretty detailed."

"That's fine. That'll give me time to do the research." I nodded, mind racing. "I think I'll have an Arnold Palmer after all."

Mac rubbed his hands together, grinning, and escorted me back to the bar.

I slid onto an empty stool next to Ferris and leaned across him to speak to Ford. "Jim Carter dug a trench today for the new statues. You know, the ones Terry delivered Wednesday." Maybe I could divert Ford's interest from the wooden African statues to the much larger, as-yet-unseen, *Wind in the Willows* statues. "A gravel truck's coming tomorrow at seven thirty in the morning. I was going to go out and watch. You interested?"

"Sure," Ford said. He jerked his thumb toward Ferris. "This is Ferris."

"We've met." I shook Ferris's proffered hand. It was callused but spongy. "Any luck?"

Mac set my tea-and-lemonade mix on the counter. A maraschino cherry floated in the ice.

Ferris shrugged. "Talked to a couple foremen. They said the real money's in construction, not maintenance."

"There are several wind farms being built upriver." I took a sip.

The subject of statues seemed to be over. I couldn't undo what Ford had said, and to bring it up again would just make a lasting impression in people's minds. No—better to let the topic pass and hope no one paid it any more attention.

I was glad to see Ferris being sociable. Maybe I'd caught him at a bad moment at the campground.

"Do you enjoy rural living?" I asked. "Wind farms aren't usually near civilization."

"Yeah, you could say that. You from around here, originally?"

"No. Lived in Vancouver and worked in Portland up until two years ago."

"Any of your friends come visit you up here?"

"Not really. They're city people. Wouldn't know what to do with themselves without a Starbucks and yoga classes," I replied.

Mac was back at our end of the bar and heard my comment. "I thought that guy driving the red Corvette was a friend of yours—the one who's staying at Gloria's place." He leaned on his palms on the counter, way too interested for my taste.

I gritted my teeth. "He's not a friend. Just an acquaintance."

"Must know you pretty well to come all the way out here," Ferris said.

Mac hurried away to swap a full glass for an empty one farther down the bar.

"Yeah, well, he's leaving."

Ferris twirled his glass in its condensation ring.

"Hey, Meredith." Val—once again pink and sparkly—slid onto the stool next to me.

"Val! I'm so glad. I heard—well, anyway—I heard." I didn't want to mention Val's imprisonment and release in front of everyone.

"Yeah," Val nodded. "Sheriff Marge was real nice. And Ham, too, in his way. He's arranging for a few repairs at the store. We're leaving in the morning."

"Together?"

"Oh, no. Definitely not. I could go now—I just wasn't up to facing my parents yet. I'll bite the bullet tomorrow. At least Rosie will understand."

"Your dog?"

Val's forehead wrinkled. "Yeah. My parents thought Ham was a sure thing for me. They won't be happy to find out what I did, and that he's not in the picture anymore."

"I know what that's like."

"Really?"

"Oh, yeah. He had—still has—my mother and stepfather bamboozled. They think the sun rises and sets with him and just don't understand why I wouldn't want to date a two-timing schmoozer."

Val giggled.

"Where are you staying?"

"With Betty Jenkins. Sheriff Marge arranged it."

"Betty's a sweetheart. Greg, my intern, stays with her when he's working at the museum. Has she baked cookies for you yet?"

Ferris tossed a few bills on the counter, nodded to us, and left.

"Snickerdoodles and apricot bars."

Mac was making the rounds and skidded to a stop in front of us.

I pounced on the moment. "Val, you should meet Mac MacDougal—owner of this establishment and master woodworker. He builds the most gorgeous display cases for the museum."

Mac, clearly smitten, stood with his mouth open.

Val stuck out her hand. "Valerie Brown, lately incarcerated for hitting my ex-boyfriend with a soup can."

Mac revived enough to grasp her fingers. "Wow." He beamed.

"And it's good night for me," I said. I patted Ford's arm. "See you in the morning."

I glanced over my shoulder before pushing through the front door. Val was talking, fluttering her hands in the air, while Mac gazed at her, riveted. I grinned.

CHAPTER 10

Clutching an insulated mug of coffee and milk sweetened with brown sugar in one hand—my Chevy Cheyenne pickup came off the assembly line before cup holders were invented—I spun the steering wheel toward the Imogene's access road with my free hand. Living sling-less felt so good.

The overcast cloud layer was just beginning to lighten in the east. It would be another fine day of drizzle. Better than ice, though. I'd slept very little with the thrumming racket of the fans vibrating the RV last night. Hence the need for an extra-large dose of caffeine.

Intentionally early, I was hoping to wrap up a few loose ends and check if Mr. Rittenour had returned my call before the gravel truck arrived. But a shiny red Corvette waited in the parking lot.

I muttered under my breath. Why wouldn't he just go away? *Marvin K. Mooney Will You Please Go Now!*—the Dr. Seuss title popped into my head. That was exactly how I felt about Ham. Except in the end, Mr. Mooney gets the point. Ham still hadn't.

I pulled in next to the Corvette and noticed it was empty. Ham wasn't a nature lover. Why would he be wandering the grounds, and at this time of day?

I slid out of the truck and pulled my jacket snug. The breeze rippled my hair. Maybe another storm was blowing in.

I scanned the park—the gray-green lawn and dark trees, the silvery river, the looming, boxy mansion. No sign of a man walking. Unless he was on the far side of the museum, but why would he go there? I leaned against the truck and sipped my coffee. Well, if Ham wanted to try his persuasive charms again, he could find me. But his efforts would return void—guaranteed.

Mud, river water, maybe a little algae and some rotting leaves—the wind mingled the hints and notes, and I inhaled. Even rain has an odor—fresh or astringent, depending on what it dampens. This combination—it's the scent of my freedom. And I'd never give that up.

Jim would arrive in a few minutes, so I decided to skip getting a head start on my work and instead ambled toward the new excavation. It was a good thing the gravel was going in today—it would help keep the mud to a minimum with more rain coming. I hoped the edges of the trench hadn't caved in overnight.

I slipped in the mucky grass and held my mug out so coffee wouldn't slosh on my jacket.

The trench was the darkest thing in sight—and several feet deep. In the dim light, it looked even more like an extra-long, curved version of Bard's grave. *It's just a hole,* I told myself.

But there was something in the trench—something pale. I squinted and leaned closer, careful not to stand on the very edge lest it crumble under me. A hand? It looked like a white hand.

Now I picked out the form—legs, torso, one arm stretched out, ending in the hand. All in dark clothing. And where the head should be—dark hair. It—he?—was lying facedown.

A spot of red caught my eye. A bunch of flowers—roses.

My stomach dropped.

Had Ham gone for a walk and fallen in? The roses—were they another attempt to change my mind? Of all the stupid things to do.

I slid down the bank and nudged him with my toe. "You okay?"

I knelt and put a hand on his shoulder. As soon as I touched him, I knew.

"No. No, no, no. What have you done?"

He was incredibly heavy, but I pulled his shoulder and head up and wrestled his face toward me. His eyes stared back, wide in terror, his mouth open as if he meant to yell.

I dropped him and let out a muffled whimper.

Out. I had to get out of the trench.

This wasn't real. It wasn't happening. I'd wake up in a minute.

I scrabbled frantically in the mud, clawing at the trench wall.

"Whoa. What's this? You fall in?" Strong hands grabbed my arms and hauled me up.

Another face—Jim's—blurred in front of me, but my mind replaced it with Ham's horrified expression. I shook my head. "Dead. He's dead."

"Who's dead?" Jim held me steady, his frown deepening. He moved me aside and peered into the trench. Casting a worried glance back at me, he eased into the hole and picked up Ham's hand, feeling for a pulse. He tried to flex Ham's fingers, and when they wouldn't move, he set the hand down gently.

In the increasing light, streaks of color were now visible—a blue stripe on Ham's jacket, his tan shoes. The red roses stood out in relief.

I moaned.

"Okay," Jim said. He kicked a toehold in the trench wall and hoisted himself out in an instant. He wrapped an arm tight around me.

He walked me to his truck, opened the passenger door, and helped me climb in.

I stared through the windshield in a daze. Ham of the crooked grin. Ham the obnoxious, persistent, irritating, boyish, handsome—

Jim settled in the driver's seat, started the engine, and turned on the heater. He leaned across the center console and touched my arm.

I blinked back tears.

Jim shook my arm. "Meredith!" he shouted.

I winced and looked at him.

"Can you hear me? You're in shock."

I nodded.

"What's his name?" Jim started dialing his cell phone.

"Ham."

He stopped and frowned at me.

"Hamilton Wexler."

He finished dialing and held the phone to his ear. A dump truck full of gravel rumbled into the parking lot, the driver downshifting, then the brakes squealing to a stop. The racket drowned Jim's voice, but I knew he was talking to Sheriff Marge.

I hunkered in Jim's truck, bent at the waist, forehead resting on the dash, arms sandwiched between my stomach and thighs. I knew what the sheriff's deputies would do when they arrived, and I didn't want to see it.

Jim checked on me a couple of times, squeezed my shoulder, but didn't say anything. Good man.

Raindrops pattered the cab's roof, and I shivered.

My thoughts spread like buckshot. I didn't try to reel them in or force them into coherency. Scenes from my old life—my ambitious, professional, girlfriend-then-fiancée-of-a-rising-young-deputy-prosecutor life—flitted across my mind's screen. There'd been fun times, even good times. Arlene, Ham's mother, was a kind woman and had made me feel like family. She and I had traipsed through home-and-garden shows together and visited Portland's celebrated rose and rhododendron gardens during blooming seasons.

I groaned. Someone would have to tell Arlene.

A white Freightliner Sprinter arrived, driven by a medical examiner's technician. It bumped across the lawn and parked near the trench.

The dump truck left, still full.

What had Ham been doing? Why had he been at the museum at all? Val had said he was leaving this morning, but he wasn't normally such an early bird.

The door opened, letting in a blast of cold air. Sheriff Marge in her clear plastic poncho and hat cover. She heaved a sigh. "Rough day."

I nodded dumbly.

"I need you to tell me when you last saw your cell phone."

"When I—why?"

Sheriff Marge tipped her head. "Humor me."

"I think yesterday—when I called the gallery—well, the CPA firm. When you told me to use the museum line instead. I put it in my purse after that, and it's still there."

"No, it's not." Sheriff Marge held up a plastic bag containing a muddy cell phone.

I scowled.

"This is yours. I checked the number."

"But—can I—I just want to look in my purse."

Sheriff Marge moved out of the way.

I hurried to my truck, pulled my purse—a tote bag, really, I carry so much stuff—across the bench seat, and rummaged through it, checked the pockets. Then I dumped it out.

I turned to Sheriff Marge, who stood waiting. "It *is* gone."

Sheriff Marge always looked worried, but there was something else—a deeper concern—behind her gray eyes now.

"Where was it?"

"Under Ham's body."

"My phone was under Ham's body?" I repeated, not believing. "Why? How?"

"Exactly."

I swallowed. What did it mean? Someone must have taken my phone. When? Who?

I swallowed again. "How did he die?"

"Stabbed. Three slashes, fast and deep, with a hunting knife. The knife was still in him."

"I didn't see—"

"Down low. The last stab was in his abdomen." Sheriff Marge paused as Ford joined us.

His shoulders were slumped, and his raincoat was bunched around his neck. His hands were wedged deep in his pockets.

"What's wrong, Ford?" I asked, then shuddered. Everything was wrong.

"I'm sorry for ya, Missus Morehouse. Just wanted to say so."

"Thanks. I know."

He shuffled away, and we watched until he rounded the corner of the museum.

"What'd you do last night?" Sheriff Marge asked.

"Uh, I went to Mac's after work, stayed for maybe an hour. Then I went home and went to bed early—about nine thirty—since I knew it would be a short night and I'm sleeping on the couch."

"Yeah, I heard about the ice damage to your trailer. See anyone between leaving Mac's and this morning?"

"Just Tuppence."

"How about at Mac's? Who'd you talk to?"

"Well, Mac, of course. He showed me a new display-case prototype, which is why I went in the first place. Ford was there, and Ferris—he's staying at the campground, too. Then Val came in. I was glad to see her—seems like she's doing better. That's it."

"Val was still there when you left?"

"Yeah, they all were. Oh, except Ferris. He left a few minutes before I did."

Sheriff Marge nodded. "I know you've been having some disagreements with Ham. What was your last interaction like, and when was it?"

"Yesterday morning, here—in my office, shortly after you left. The conversation was the same from his end—talking without listening, trying to persuade me to consider his proposal. But I told him no—clearly and firmly—for the first time. I was actually able to say it, and then I told him—" I faltered.

Sheriff Marge raised her eyebrows.

I shifted my gaze, stared at a dripping laurel bush without seeing it. "I told him to go away," I whispered. "That was the last thing I said to him." I pressed my palms to my eyes.

"All right. I'll have more questions later. We've already cordoned off the whole parking lot because we need to take a look at the car." Sheriff Marge nodded in the Corvette's direction. "You can go home, but I don't want you leaving the county."

"What? I mean, I don't plan to—but why?"

"Because you have motive, means, and no alibi."

"But I didn't—I wouldn't—" I clenched my hands. "Everyone knows I didn't like him, but I wouldn't—I don't own a hunting knife." I looked straight into Sheriff Marge's steady gray eyes. "I *found* him."

Sheriff Marge grasped my shoulder. "I put everyone on my suspect list. Then I narrow it down. That's how I work. Now, go on—I'll come see you later."

Numb, I climbed into my truck and went through the motions of driving. At the end of the parking lot, Dale gave me a solemn nod and lifted the yellow crime scene tape. It slid across the windshield as I rolled under it.

CHAPTER 11

I nosed the pickup into the short drive in front of my fifth-wheel trailer and slumped in the seat. Rain rivulets meandered down the windshield—merging, separating into new channels, trickling away the minutes. I submerged, lumpish, into a void, an absence of thought.

Ham's face—pale, almost translucent skin, dark petrified eyes, and mouth stretched wide—wavered inside my eyelids and jolted me out of my stupor. The cab had chilled. My skin was clammy.

I bolted from the truck and hurried into the trailer, clicking the door firmly closed behind me. My breath came in bursts. I needed a solid, warm dog to hold.

But Tuppence hadn't greeted me. She was probably still off on her morning rounds, checking to see if anything had changed in the night.

Changed in the night. I hung my head. My whole body felt weak, boneless. I dropped to the couch. What I really needed was Pete. He'd just hold me and not talk. I wanted to time my heartbeats with his and be still. But the tug was probably already under way. And I couldn't even call him, because my phone was evidence.

I burrowed into the cushions and pulled a wad of blankets over my head.

A soft whining outside woke me. And rustling.

I got up and opened the door. A blast of eye-watering, searing skunk odor nearly bowled me over.

"Ugh." I pulled my shirt collar up over my nose and mouth.

Tuppence wriggled on the welcome mat and whined pitifully. She rubbed her nose with first one front paw and then the other.

I grabbed my keys and hurried down the steps. Tuppence tried to rub on my legs.

"No, no. Not right now. I'll be back as soon as I can. That's a good girl. Just hold on."

I sped to Junction General and flew through the store collecting paper towels, hydrogen peroxide, baking soda, dish soap, and sponges.

"Tuppence get into a skunk?" Gloria asked when I dumped everything on the counter.

"You can tell from my purchases?"

"Yes. But I can smell it, too."

"Sorry. She barely touched me."

Gloria loaded the supplies into a paper bag. "Winter skunk is worse than summer skunk."

I handed her a couple of bills. "Why is that?"

"It's not scientific, just my opinion. Skunks don't truly hibernate, but they do sleep a lot in the winter. They have to come out at least once to empty their scent sacs. I think the oil—you know, what's been stored for a month or two—has to be even stronger."

"Eeew."

"Hey." Gloria placed a hand on mine. "I heard there was a murder at the museum and that it's Ham."

I nodded and held my breath.

"He had paid to stay through today, but when his car wasn't here this morning, I figured he left early. So I went upstairs to clean—"

A furrow deepened in Gloria's forehead. "His things are still here—toothbrush and shaving kit, clothes. His laptop's on the dining table. I ducked out quickly because I thought maybe he was coming back in a few minutes, but now—"

I exhaled. The part about my finding Ham's body apparently hadn't made the gossip chain yet. "You did right. I'm sure Sheriff Marge will want to have a look around." I scooped up the sack and hustled toward the exit.

"I'm really sorry since he was your friend," Gloria called.

"Thanks," I mumbled as I pushed the door open with my behind and spun into the parking lot.

ooo

I rolled Tuppence on her back and pinned her down. The skunk had sprayed the dog squarely on the chest, and the spray extended under her chin and across her front legs. There was oil on the ends of her ears, too. I dabbed at the concentrated areas with paper towels and tried not to inhale. My eyes streamed.

Tuppence struggled and whined.

"I know. Just hold still, okay? Please?"

I released the dog, and Tuppence slid into the grass and rolled and rolled.

"No, no, no. You're spreading it around. Our whole campsite is going to reek." I groaned.

Too late.

"Come here." I patted my leg.

Tuppence returned, and I worked the foaming solution of hydrogen peroxide, baking soda, and dish soap into the hound's fur. I rubbed the sponge in firm, circular motions until Tuppence's front half was solid lather. Then I rinsed the dog with the hose.

Tuppence shook—a spin cycle that started with her nose and ears and worked its way along her lanky frame to the tip of her tail.

"Okay. Again. This time all of you."

I worked the dog over with the scent-diluting solution until Tuppence looked like a poodle. This time she shook before being rinsed and splattered bits of lather all over a ten-foot radius. I sprayed her off, then aimed the soaked dog toward clean grass and let her roll.

I examined my polka-dotted clothes. They would never smell laundry-fresh again. I didn't want to wear them inside because the skunk oil would spread to whatever it touched. Glancing around furtively, I sidled to the back of the trailer—the most sheltered side. No boats in view on the river. The campground seemed to be deserted.

I stripped off my clothes—all of them. They were soaked through, and the skunk oil would have traveled with the water, all the way to my skin.

Realizing I'd never streaked before—there's a first time for everything—I darted around the trailer, leaped over the welcome mat, scrambled up the stairs, and flung myself inside the trailer. Olympic medal–worthy.

I beelined for the shower and washed my hair three times. Hot water pelted until my fingertips turned pruny. I toweled off, dressed, and pulled a large trash bag from under the kitchen sink. Using only my thumb and forefinger, I collected and dropped my ruined clothing and the welcome mat into the plastic trash bag and tied it closed. Tuppence followed me to the dumpster.

"Well," I said, "have you learned? Are you going to leave skunks alone now?"

Tuppence snorted.

"I don't think I believe you."

Sheriff Marge was waiting at the trailer when we returned. She cleared her throat. "Looks like I missed the excitement."

I wrinkled my nose. "I guess I've gotten used to it. I mean, I smell skunk, but how bad is it—really?"

"Pungent."

"I don't think Tuppence'll smell quite as bad when she dries."

"How about you?"

"I'm hoping the same."

Sheriff Marge chuckled. It started in the middle of her belly and jiggled outward, like ripples spreading from a stone dropped in a puddle. Her Kevlar vest had a dampening effect on her top half.

"Hah," she sighed. She removed her hat and plunked it on the Explorer's hood, then leaned over the hood and propped her elbows beside her hat.

"It's bad. I know," I said.

"The skunk or the murder?"

"Both. Plus the domestic with the suicide, and whatever else you've been working on that I don't know about. Want coffee?"

Sheriff Marge pushed off the SUV. "Yeah."

We didn't speak again until we were settled across from each other at the dining table with steaming mugs cradled in our hands.

"Am I still a suspect?" I asked.

"Yeah."

I exhaled and leaned back. "What do you need to know?"

"Just walk me through your evening again."

I complied. It was so uneventful I finished in a couple of minutes.

"Did Ham have enemies?"

"I'm sure he did. As a deputy prosecutor, he helped put many unsavory characters behind bars. They'd all have a reason not to like him. Did you talk to Val? She'd have a better idea of his recent trials and people he interacted with because of his campaign."

"Yeah. She's on my list, too."

"Val? Oh, I suppose—soup can, hunting knife." I chuckled. "I don't believe it. She's so tiny, and I thought she was really over him."

"She's strong for her size. If the victim is unsuspecting and doesn't put up a fight—you just have to get the knife in the right places, which the murderer did."

"You mean Ham didn't fight back?"

"There are a couple small defensive wounds, but no, he didn't really. Possibly because it was fast and over quickly."

"When did it happen?"

"Between ten and eleven last night."

"While I was sleeping—or trying to sleep." I motioned toward the couch and rumpled pile of blankets. "I don't understand why he was on the museum grounds. Even if he wanted to talk to me, he'd know I wasn't there that time of night."

"Because you sent him a text."

"What?"

Sheriff Marge pulled her notebook out of her pocket and flipped it open. "'I've been thinking about what you said and need to see you. Working late tonight. Meet me in front of the museum.'"

My jaw dropped. "But I didn't text him. It's on my phone?"

Sheriff Marge nodded.

"What time was it sent?"

Sheriff Marge checked her notes. "At 9:36 p.m."

I slumped forward, elbows on the table, chin in my hands. "Were there fingerprints on the phone?"

"No. Too smeared with mud. None on the knife, either."

"Have you talked to Gloria? She said his laptop's still in the apartment. Maybe something in his e-mail would provide clues."

"Dale's working on that now."

"So someone knew about Ham and me and what was going on between us and used that to lure Ham to his death?"

"Who could have stolen your phone?"

"I lock my office at night, but not during the day while I'm at the museum. We have so few visitors that I never worried about it. I know I left my office a couple times during the day, so someone could have walked in and taken it then. Lindsay'll have a visitor count, but we don't know their names unless they used a credit card to pay admission.

I talked with Jim outside, went to the tavern, came home. The tavern was getting crowded when I left."

"In other words, just about anyone had access."

I sighed. "Yeah, but why? I guess you could say Val and I have similar motives since we both dated him at some point. I was trying to keep him away, and she was trying to keep him close. But is that enough to kill him—really? There has to be another reason."

Sheriff Marge shoved back from the table and stood. "Do you have contact info for his next of kin?"

"Yeah—Arlene, his mom." I flipped open my laptop and pulled up Arlene's phone number and address.

"What about a dad?"

"Died when Ham was thirteen. My stepfather mentored him through college and law school."

Sheriff Marge's eyebrows shot up.

"It's complicated."

"I always wondered why you don't seem to talk to your family much."

"Ham was the breaking point. But it started long before that. They maintain a smooth finish—pretend they and the few people they're close to don't have problems. I always asked too many questions and didn't like the answers I got."

"Are you going to call them now?"

"I'm a suspect."

"Right. I'll arrange for his mother to be notified."

ooo

I gave up trying to sleep long before dawn. Ham's phantom face kept appearing in the darkness, frozen in terror. I shuddered and flung off the blankets.

Val couldn't have done it. I thought back to the episode at Junction General. Ham had been calm, measured, reasoning. He hadn't been terrified of Val.

No, his face had been the stuff of nightmares—*his* nightmares. What had he been afraid of?

I stumbled to the dining table and fired up the laptop. Two hours later I still didn't have an idea of what kind of menace Ham might have reason to fear. I'd searched for his name and read all the articles I could find relating to trials he'd been involved with. Some I remembered from when we were dating, and I learned more from the news accounts than I'd ever learned from him. He'd been better than I knew at leaving the dirty stuff at work.

Murderers, rapists, drug dealers, blackmailers, embezzlers—it was all there. But there were very few controversial cases, in which the innocence of the defendant was a hotly contested possibility. Defense tactics usually fall in the he-shouldn't-be-held-accountable-for-his-actions category. The majority of criminals accept plea deals, and those rarely make the news. Most prosecutors know better than to take cases to trial without overwhelming evidence—unless they're politically motivated.

Ham's landmark case—the one flaunted all over his campaign website—was the successful prosecution of a cop-killer, Ozzie Fulmer. The trial had occurred during my third year of college, but I remembered the late-night strategy sessions Ham and my stepfather held in the den over Christmas break—whiteboard easels, flip charts, ideal jury profiles, and a careful orchestration of media presence. Even then, early in his career, Ham had excelled at manipulating the press. Although for this case it hadn't really been necessary. The public, and the members of the jury selected from it, were dead set against Fulmer. He was convicted and sentenced to life in prison, no chance of parole—even though Fulmer claimed he'd been set up and kept his story straight throughout the proceedings.

As Terry had pointed out, the best alibi is incarceration. Fulmer was still making license plates at the Washington State Penitentiary in Walla Walla and couldn't be Ham's murderer.

A deep hollowness weighed on me. In my high school and early college years, I'd been infatuated with Ham, hoping someday he'd notice his mentor's shy stepdaughter. Then he did, and I loved him—or thought I did—then hated him, then tried to convince myself I was ambivalent toward him by moving away and starting a new life. His unexpected reappearance had made me realize I still disliked him, and now what?

Now I felt sorry for him. He'd certainly run me through the gamut of emotions. I shivered and rubbed my arms.

Tuppence sneezed under the trailer, in exile until the skunk scent faded—poor dog.

I took a rawhide treat outside.

The dog thumped her tail and whined.

"I know, and I'm sorry. I'll give you another bath this afternoon." I tousled Tuppence's ears.

I returned to the warmth of the trailer and started the coffeemaker.

Sunday. What would people think if a murder suspect showed up at church smelling faintly of skunk? One way to find out. I was starving to hear some good news.

CHAPTER 12

The organist was warming up when I slid into a back pew at Platts Landing Bible Church. I'd only had to shake two hands and accept a bulletin on the way in—no accusatory glances or uncomfortable questions. I turned to smile politely at the man seated a few feet farther in and stared for a few moments before recognizing him without the Stetson—Julian.

"Hi. How are you?" I scooted closer. Ham was not the first dead body I'd seen. Bard, Julian's son, had been the first, a couple of months ago.

Julian nodded. "All right. You? I heard." His golden eyes bored into mine.

"I don't know."

The congregation rustled and rose for the opening hymn. A sweet melody filled the small chapel. I closed my eyes and let the music ripple over me like water.

Pastor Mort preached from the end of the book of Jude—about glory, majesty, power, and authority—with enthusiastic gestures, his face animated. *He loves his job,* I thought, *probably because he loves his God. And Mort would say he loves God because God loved him first—that no person is lovable in and of themselves, no one is deserving.* I had often thought that was true of others—people who caused hurt, like Ham. But now that he was gone—well, I was no saint, either.

Sally found me afterward, hugged me tight, and pulled me aside. "I heard. I'm so sorry—I'm so sorry."

My faint smile wobbled.

"Not able to sleep?"

"No."

Sally rubbed my arm. "It takes a while, I know. And I've never found someone—well, under the circumstances you did. Just natural causes for me."

"That many?"

"Everyone seems to want a pastor when they're dying—if not for them, then for the family. Mort gets called a lot, and I go with him if I can. It's nice for them to have someone to talk to, someone who's been through it before. But it's usually for old people or people who've been ill for a while. You need anything?"

I shook my head.

"I could bring a casserole over."

I laughed. "I have enough food. But thank you."

"Are you coming to the potluck?" Sally meant the Sunday-afternoon football-watching community potluck at Mac's tavern.

"No. I think I've maxed out my sociability for today."

Sally gave me another squeeze. "You need anything at all, you call, okay? Anything."

When I was halfway to my truck, a firm hand gripped my elbow. I turned.

"Got busy in there. But I wanted to talk with you," Julian said, Stetson now squarely on his head.

My arm extended awkwardly because Julian still held it, and I returned a step. Julian moved his hand to my shoulder. I couldn't bring myself to look away. Once his eyes locked on—but they were gentler than usual today.

"Did you love him?" he asked.

I dropped my head. Everyone assumed Ham and I had been friends, even hinted around at something more. No one had asked about love. But Julian would know to probe the pain more deeply—he'd lost both his wife and his only son.

"No—maybe. Once." I sighed. "Not anymore. But when you know they're gone for good, then, well, you start wondering about what could have been." I shook my head and looked up at him. "But I shouldn't let myself think about that, should I?"

"It's better if you don't." His arm encircled my shoulders, pulled me in. I relaxed against him, weary of standing on my own two feet.

"I'm on the suspect list," I whispered.

"Sheriff Marge will figure it out. Don't worry."

"He was afraid. His face—seeing whoever did it—he was terrified." I shuddered. Then I pulled away. "I'm sorry. This must bring up memories for you—not even distant enough to be memories yet, are they?"

"There are certain scenes I still see every time I close my eyes."

I nodded. I had my scenes now, too.

"What do you need?"

"Nothing. But thank you."

"You sure you don't need a casserole? I can make Hamburger Helper," he said, surprising a laugh out of me. "You passed a whole lot of casserole on to me before. I'm just looking to return the favor."

"The thing is—I've already had several offers. Sally's trumps yours." I grinned.

He held my elbow again, serious. "But if anything comes up, if you think of anything—call."

"I will."

On the drive home, I remembered I couldn't call Sally or Julian even if I wanted to. Sheriff Marge had my muddy phone in an evidence bag. Then I wondered if anyone had tried to call me since the murder.

While looping through the campground toward my spot, I slowed at the tent area and pulled onto the shoulder. Thinking Ferris might enjoy the community potluck, I hopped out of the truck. He could go stag, without a hot dish, because everyone else always brought more than enough food.

I waded through wet, calf-high grass. Herb and Harriet Tinsley, the elderly twins who owned the campground, were letting the grass return to its native state except in the immediate vicinity of my trailer. I'm usually the only occupant during the off-season, and the twins fuss around my campsite, keeping it tidy. It makes me feel like I live on the green of a one-hole golf course. I should probably apologize for the skunk odor, although the twins' farmhouse is far enough away that they probably hadn't noticed it yet.

"Ferris?" I called, rounding the privacy hedge. "Oh." I stopped short.

The blue Datsun pickup was gone. A folded lawn chair was tipped against the picnic table and a cooler sat underneath. The campfire ring held pale ashes and a few small chunks of charred wood. Someone else must have already told him about the potluck. They wouldn't be able to stand the thought of a newcomer's not being invited. Welcome to Platts Landing, eat with us—a package deal.

I realized I'd just experienced the friendly compulsion to invite Ferris—what *they* did. Did that mean I was one of them now? Truly a member of the small community? Apparently. It felt good.

I swung my arms while striding back to the truck, inhaling the loamy scent of sodden grass and dirt. A song sparrow *chirr-twirl-chirchir-twillup-tweep-tweep*ed from a pine bough overhead.

Grilled cheese sandwich or dog bath first?

Grilled cheese.

After the bath we'd both smell strongly of skunk until we were dry again, and skunk didn't improve the flavor of melted Colby jack and toasted sourdough. Mmm. Maybe a slice of tomato, too.

ooo

After washing Tuppence, I flopped on the couch and switched on the television for the ubiquitous Sunday-afternoon football game. Maybe I could zone out.

Instead I remembered what Ford had said to me yesterday morning. "I'm sorry for ya, Missus Morehouse. Just wanted to say so."

What was Ford sorry about?

Had he assumed Ham and I were friends, like everyone else in town? Was he sorry my friend was dead?

Not only is Ford physically strong, but he also has a clearly defined moral stance. Every once in a while, he'll verbalize his views on right and wrong. I smiled at the memory of him adamantly informing Pete about the consequences of gambling. Pete had been joking, but Ford had been dead serious.

The uncomfortable idea that maybe Ford had been protecting me in some way crossed my mind. Could he have overheard me talking to Ham? Telling Ham to leave?

Ford had been going to meet me to watch the gravel delivery yesterday morning. When had he arrived? Where had he been before he spoke to me?

Ford lived on the museum grounds. Had he heard or seen something? Become curious and ventured out to investigate on Friday night?

He wouldn't have stolen my phone and sent a text. But what if he'd stumbled upon Ham? Or a struggle between Ham and someone else? Could he have accidentally killed Ham?

I moaned. I didn't want to think about that.

CHAPTER 13

Monday morning a blinking red light greeted me as I opened my office door. I dropped my purse on the chair, picked up the phone, and punched in the code to hear my voice mail.

"Ms. Morehouse, this is Earl Rittenour. Thanks for calling. I was getting anxious about the shipment. And I'm sorry to trouble you with the delivery mix-up. I'd like to handle it myself from here since the freight company seems to be unreliable. I could rent a U-Haul truck and come pick up the crates this weekend—at your earliest convenience. Please call me back at this number."

The phone beeped and played the next message.

"Uh, Ms. Morehouse. I'm sorry to bother you, but I'm a little worried I haven't heard back from you. I realize the museum may be closed for the weekend. It is a matter of some urgency, as you can imagine. The crates are—well, I need to know if they're secure. I'm sure you know how sensitive artifacts can be—humidity and whatnot. Please return my call just as soon as possible. Earl Rittenour. Thank you."

And another.

Doubled Up

"I looked up the Imogene's website—it says you're open Saturdays. Really hoping you'll get back to me soon. It's extremely urgent. I know I keep saying that, but—" A woman's voice, discontentment evident in the high, whiny pitch, sounded in the background. "Call me back," Earl muttered, and disconnected.

I wrinkled my nose. Another one.

"Sorry about that earlier message, Ms. Morehouse. I just wanted to apologize. Family vacation's getting, well, a little stressful. We didn't go anywhere—we're home, so I could come anytime to get the crates. If I don't hear from you, I'm planning to drive up Tuesday when the museum is open—I see you're closed Sundays and Mondays—and hope someone can help me. Anyway, hope to talk with you soon."

I moved my bag and sat. I poked more buttons and checked the times of Earl's calls. The first one had come just a few minutes after I'd left Friday afternoon. Then later Friday evening, Saturday morning, and Saturday afternoon. Apparently he hadn't picked up on the fact that I had the contents of only one of his crates, since he kept mentioning *crates*, plural. Maybe it was just as well.

He couldn't have known that on this particular Saturday, the museum hadn't been open. "Temporarily closed due to murder. Please come again" was not the sort of thing to post on a tourist-attraction website.

I slipped down to the chamber pot exhibit and checked the toilet tank. Eight rods present and accounted for. I wondered if Earl knew about the gold or was inexplicably enamored with ugly carvings. If he already owned some wooden statues, as his secretary had mentioned, did those come with gold inserts, too? As a CPA, he must have an inkling of what kind of mess that could get him into.

I quickly returned to my office and dialed Sheriff Marge.

"Earl Rittenour wants to pick up his statues as soon as possible. He said he's coming tomorrow if he doesn't hear back from me. Do we want that?"

"Rats. I don't know. I'm headed into the office to meet with the feds now. I can't babysit them and conduct a murder investigation." The Explorer's engine roared as Sheriff Marge stomped on the gas. "I'll get back to you."

I set the phone in its cradle. Sheriff Marge drove everywhere at breakneck speed. One of these days she was going to be the reason for an ambulance callout. I rubbed my temples.

Mondays are supposed to be one of my days off, but they're often my favorite day to work—when the museum is quiet and I have the place to myself. I opened my laptop, stared at the screen, then closed it. There would be no concentration today.

Noticing a book sticking out on the shelf opposite, I walked around my desk and pushed it in. Why was a book on French porcelain next to one about Minton majolica? Suddenly my organizational system seemed all wrong.

When I was well into the fourth bookcase, a loud voice announced my name. I jumped, bumped my head on a shelf, and backed out of the corner where I knelt. A precarious pile of books slid, domino style, across the floor until the desk leg stopped them.

"Hmm?" I rubbed my head and turned.

Sheriff Marge stood in the doorway, hands on hips, glaring over the tops of her reading glasses. "What are you doing?"

"Organizing. Cleaning."

Two men in suits peered around Sheriff Marge's hat.

"Oh." I rose to my feet, straddling another book Pisa tower.

"Lindsay let us in."

"Lindsay's here?"

"Said it was quieter than at home."

"Oh." I nodded. "College application. And, uh—" I tipped my head so Sheriff Marge would remember her guests.

Sheriff Marge jerked her thumb behind her. "Agent George Simmons, FBI, and Wayne Tubman, Treasury."

I stretched to shake hands with each man.

"Do you have a place to talk?" Sheriff Marge asked, scanning the stacks of books covering the floor in a perfect grid, like an urban development plan.

"Just a minute." I bent and rapidly doubled and tripled up stacks to clear space.

I straightened, flushed, and pushed unruly brown curls out of my face. "Sorry, we don't have a conference room. It's either sit on the bed in the chamber pot room or sit here. I'll just"—I squeezed past the men in the doorway—"get some chairs."

When I returned with three folding chairs from a storage room, I found the FBI man inspecting my empty bookcases. Sheriff Marge shrugged in response to my inquiring look.

"Here you go." I handed out chairs, and my visitors unfolded them and sat, thigh to thigh, in the cleared space. Sheriff Marge folded her arms across her chest and scowled. I slid into the chair behind my desk.

The Treasury man, I'd already forgotten his name, was older, his charcoal-colored hair lightly salted. His coif was perfectly sculpted, with an arrow-straight side part and a swoop over his forehead. It seemed to be shellacked in place—he looked like Clark Kent at fifty. He cleared his throat. "We understand you have some undeclared gold and—"

"Artifacts of possible historical significance," FBI butted in. He was heavily freckled, with a paprika-colored buzz cut that was probably a carryover from a military career. His one obvious flamboyance—Andy Rooney eyebrows. But in red they looked more like Bozo the Clown's.

There was a jostling undercurrent in the navy-suited men. Somehow, while perched stiffly on their chairs, they gave the impression they were jabbing each other with elbows and knees like jockeys in a horse race, trying to shoulder ahead. There wasn't actual movement; the competition was in their posture and tone of voice. Subtle, but the tension of their rivalry filled the room.

I nodded slowly. "I have them, but they're not mine. I agreed with Sheriff Marge to—"

"I need to see them," Superman said.

I pushed away from the desk. "I'll be right back."

I retrieved the statues first, then loaded the gold bars into the tote bag, sliding them to the bottom. The bag strained at the seams with the weight, so I wrapped my arms under it and balanced it like a sleeping toddler against my chest.

The men stood upon my arrival, but quickly sat again when they saw it was just a dirty old tote bag. I eased my burden onto the desk and opened the flap. I lifted out the statues first and laid them in a row on the desk, then handed a gold bar to Superman.

Eyebrows's fingers twitched as though he was about to snatch the bar from Superman, so I handed him his own. He balanced it across his open palm, then picked up a statue with his other hand.

"Do you know the country of origin?" I asked.

"African or Australian, I expect." He pulled a small digital camera from his pocket and snapped a close-up of each statue.

I wrinkled my nose. I'd guessed that myself. So he wasn't an expert, or he wasn't giving anything away.

"You've made contact with the dealer?" Superman asked.

"Mr. Rittenour? Yes. He's expecting a call back to know when he can pick them up. He wants to come tomorrow."

"No." Eyebrows shook his head. "I need time. This room would work for the transfer."

"What?" I asked.

"It makes sense." Superman leaned forward, elbows on knees. "His point of contact is you. So you'll keep that up. We'll script a list of questions for you to ask him—all very casual, and we'll be recording. When we get what we need, we'll arrest him."

"Wednesday afternoon—two p.m. Tell Mr. Rittenour that's when he can pick up his statues," Eyebrows said.

"But—" I glanced at Sheriff Marge, who shook her head, still scowling. I turned back to the men. "Now?"

"Go ahead. Tell him—" Eyebrows pivoted toward Sheriff Marge. "Wasn't somebody murdered on the grounds here? Yeah. Use that as your excuse for the delay. It's interfering with normal museum operation or whatever."

I swallowed and picked up the phone. I shot one more glance at Sheriff Marge, who nodded this time. After dialing, I swiveled in the chair so my back faced my audience. Sounding calm and natural wasn't going to come easy, not with three sets of eyes on me.

Earl answered on the second ring.

"This is Meredith Morehouse." My voice bounced off the walls of the small room. Someone behind me had poked the speaker button. I squeezed my eyes shut and tried to picture the very worried man on the other end of the line.

"Meredith." Earl was breathless. "I'm so relieved."

"I'm awfully sorry I didn't call you sooner. The museum was closed Saturday because an unfortunate incident—well, uh, a tourist was killed—"

"What?" Earl nearly shrieked.

"Outside, on the grounds—not actually in the museum," I continued. "But we were all quite upset—I'm sure you understand—and I wasn't able to keep my normal schedule, and actually—" I took a deep breath. "It's still not back to normal—"

"Of course. Of course," Earl murmured. "Dreadful. I'm sorry."

"I was wondering—would Wednesday afternoon work for you? Around two p.m.?"

"Yes." Earl leaped to answer. "I have the directions. I'll be there."

"Ask for me at the front desk."

"All right. And thank you. Thank you very much."

"You're welcome," said the spider to the fly. I groaned inwardly. No matter how shady Earl Rittenour might be, I hated what I'd just done. I whirled around and hung up.

I took a deep breath. "He's expecting fourteen crates, which we don't have. He's already a very nervous man. The sight of a damaged semitruck and trailer at the far end of our parking lot might send him over the edge."

"You boys check the trailer this afternoon if you want, then we can release it," Sheriff Marge said.

"I need to get my crates out before it's moved," I blurted. "Jim said maybe Verle's tow truck—" I stopped, not certain about the mechanics of unloading.

Sheriff Marge stood. "We'll work it out." She slid a small black object onto my desk. "Coming, boys?"

They marched out single file.

A cell phone! I poked through the menu. Sheriff Marge had had all my contacts transferred to the new phone—all my friends. I leaned back, drew my knees to my chest, and hugged them. Bless that woman.

On a sudden impulse, I pressed the button for Arlene Wexler. I had to tell Ham's mother I was sorry—sorry about everything.

"Oh, Meredith, I'm so glad you called." Arlene sounded tired, without the usual spunk to her pleasant alto voice.

"How are you?"

"It hasn't really sunk in yet. I didn't see Ham very often anymore, with the campaign and all, but sometimes when a car drives by, I'll think it's him and hurry to the window before I remember."

I sighed. "How did they—I mean, how did you—I should have called you right away."

"It's okay, honey. A couple Clark County deputies came by—a man and a woman, I don't remember their names—and told me. They found me out back, separating daffodil bulbs, mud up to my armpits. If I wasn't a mess before, I sure was after. But they were very kind. That must be the absolute worst part of their jobs. Then Sheriff Stettler—Marge Stettler, the sheriff where you live—called, and she was very kind, too. We talked about losing our husbands for a while—" Arlene's voice trailed off.

I stared at the ceiling. I'd forgotten. Sheriff Marge is a widow, too, and would know what to say. "Did she tell you I found him?"

"Yes. She was worried about you. I wanted to talk to you, but she said you needed some time." Arlene broke down, sniffling between her words. "I don't want to make you relive it, but could you tell me—was he—" She sobbed.

I fought back my own tears. There was no way I would tell Arlene about the expression on Ham's face. "Sheriff Marge said it must have happened very fast—very quickly."

Arlene exhaled shakily. "I'm so sorry you were the one to find him. I didn't know what he planned to do, but it makes sense he wanted to see you. You were always the solid person in his life, the one who gave him purpose. He'd go off on his escapades, but he'd always return to 'What would Meredith think?' or 'Meredith would have loved that.' You were his guiding light."

I gritted my teeth. "Arlene, I—"

"I know," Arlene whispered. "You were good for him, but he wasn't good for you. No, my Ham wasn't husband material. I guess I just wanted—wanted you for my own, too. The daughter I didn't have."

"Then I'm yours. If you'll have me, I'm yours. I really need—a mother would be wonderful." Tears leaked from the corners of my scrunched-up eyes.

"There, there," Arlene murmured.

I let out a juicy half chuckle and wiped my nose on my sleeve. I took a deep breath.

"When this is over, I'm going to come visit," Arlene said. "Because that's what mothers do—pester and nag and suggest and meddle. Are you ready for that?"

"Yes." I smiled, though my vision was still watery.

CHAPTER 14

I barely had time to blow my nose before my new phone rang.

"Got your carpet."

"Oh." I sniffed. "Thanks. When—" A loud metal screech made me jerk the phone away from my ear.

"Need to fix the roof while it's not raining."

"You're at my trailer now?" I asked.

Jim sighed into the phone.

"I'm coming." I hung up and thought perhaps his wife had left him because he failed to inform her in advance of important plans. The comforting weight of the phone nestled in my palm. Maybe he *had* called and I'd missed the message.

Realizing the suits had been hustled out by Sheriff Marge before giving instructions about what to do with the gold and statues, I quickly returned them to their hiding places.

I stopped by the gift shop. "How's it going?"

Lindsay had papers spread across the counter and her laptop open. "I printed out everything for one last check, then I'm submitting the application. I made the changes you suggested." She shuffled the pages together. "Who were those guys with Sheriff Marge?"

"Um, outside agency representatives. Our county's so short-staffed, sometimes Sheriff Marge gets outside help for, uh, things."

"Well, I knew they weren't from around here." Lindsay smirked. "Suits and briefcases. And did you see the eyebrows on the red-haired guy?" She rolled her eyes. "Are they helping with the murder investigation?"

"Sheriff Marge hasn't really—I'm not sure she can—since I'm a suspect, you know." I inhaled.

"Oh, right." Lindsay nodded. "I know you didn't do it, but it must be awful to have that hanging over you. Kind of creepy, don't you think?" Her eyes darted back and forth. "Somebody did it."

"But probably not anyone we know. I think Ham was specifically targeted, possibly because he's a deputy prosecuting attorney in Clark County."

"I'm still leaving before it gets dark."

"Good idea. Call your mom, too, and let her know you're on your way."

I stopped halfway to the front doors and wheeled around. "Were there any unusual visitors Friday?"

Lindsay pursed her lips as she pulled out a beat-up spiral notebook—the visitor log. "We had twenty-eight visitors, which is a lot, especially for a winter holiday weekend." She ran her finger down the times of entry and number of people per party. "Yeah. All were families or retired couples, except—around two forty-five, two men came in together. That's sort of odd, because they clearly weren't *together*, if you know what I mean. Dudes don't usually tour museums with their buddies. But these guys did. And I mean they looked at everything—read every placard. They left just before we closed at six."

"What did they look like?"

"Jeans, sneakers. One wore a zip-up Windbreaker-type jacket. The other wore a gray hooded sweatshirt. The sweatshirt guy was pretty cute. That's another reason I know they weren't together—he kind of flirted with me."

"Hair color, eye color, any distinguishing marks?"

"Well, the cute one had short brown hair, brown eyes. His front teeth overlapped a little, not bad—probably not worth getting braces for—just, you know, kind of cute. The other guy I didn't talk to. He kept sniffing like he had allergies or something."

"Youngish?"

"Late twenties—maybe."

"Did you see what they were driving?"

"I didn't notice. Sorry."

I bit my lip and stared at the floor.

"What's wrong?"

"My phone was stolen Friday."

"We have to talk to Rupert about getting better security. This is too much, Meredith. Murder, theft—" Lindsay shook her head.

Mentally I added gold smuggling and art theft/forgery to the list.

ooo

On the drive home, I drummed my fingers on the steering wheel. The sooner the statue-and-gold problem was resolved, the better. With all the questions and suspicions flying around the museum, the truth, or the part of the truth I wasn't supposed to mention, was going to pop out of my mouth—I just knew it. Lying has never been in my skill set—at least not *successful* lying.

My campsite looked as if a single-minded tornado had passed through. The tarp had been flung over the picnic table, bungee cords scattered. Buckets, hand tools, and gloves were dumped haphazardly on the ground. Tuppence wagged expectantly at the base of a stepladder. A scraping sound came from above.

I climbed the ladder. Jim knelt on my roof, spreading thick, tarry gunk along the split seam.

"Your dog get into a skunk?" he asked.

I assumed it was a rhetorical question. "Need help?"

"Nope."

"Lunch?"

"Okay."

I unlocked the fifth-wheel's door and blocked Tuppence from entering. "Not yet, old girl. Sorry."

Most of my pantry shelves were down to the bare wood, but the old standby—bread and cheese—remained. I hoped Jim wouldn't mind eating the kind of lunch normally served to a five-year-old. While the sandwiches sizzled, I started the coffeemaker and chopped a Granny Smith apple and a few pecans for a quick Waldorf salad.

The trailer shook as Jim moved around, thumping and generally sounding as though he was about to put a foot through the ceiling. I clutched the edge of the counter for a second to steady myself, then flipped the sandwiches over.

A power tool—maybe a drill?—*whirr-whirwhirwhirr*red in a high-pitched whine. Several more loud bangs, then the ladder squeaked as Jim descended.

He opened the door and came in. "Roof's fixed." He dropped into a chair at the dining table.

"Thank you." I slid a plate and mug in front of him. "We have to remove the crates from the semitrailer at the museum in the next day. Do you think Verle—"

"Thought Sheriff Marge wouldn't want me working on the murder site till she gives the all clear."

"I'm sure that's right. But we need to store the crates somewhere else so they can move the semi."

Jim nodded, his mouth full.

I took a bite of my sandwich while standing at the kitchen island.

"You going to sit?" Jim mumbled around a wad of cheese and sourdough.

I eased onto a chair opposite him, careful not to bump his knees under the table. "Thanks for helping on Saturday when—you took care of everything, and I really appreciate it."

"You were shell-shocked."

I kept my head down and chewed.

"Well." Jim shoved his chair back and slurped the last of his coffee. "Carpet won't take long."

He hauled the fans out to his truck and returned with an unwieldy roll of confetti-colored foam under his arm—the carpet pad. I saved my mug just in time as he swiped the roll across the island counter and marched up the steps to my bedroom.

Grunting and ripping sounds, more thudding—I cringed and tidied the kitchen. I thought about offering to help, but the bedroom was too small to afford elbow room for a second, and inexperienced, carpet layer.

Jim made another trip to the truck. "Sandstorm," he announced upon returning with a second roll. "Crazy names those people come up with for brown. The other option was Teera—Tiramisu. What the heck is that? Sounds like somethin' you wouldn't want to step in."

My phone rang.

"Good, you got the phone. Thanks for going along with the feds today," Sheriff Marge said.

"Thank you. I didn't realize how much I used my phone until I didn't have it."

"I tried to call you yesterday and about scared Archie's pants off. He was in the evidence room, checking stuff in, when your phone rang in a box."

"How's the investigation going?"

"Val's clear. Betty alibied for her. Been talking with the Sidetrack Tavern patrons. The only person everyone didn't know was this Ferris, who you also mentioned. What do you know about him?"

"He's staying here at the campground. I thought maybe he went to the potluck yesterday because I stopped to check on him after church and he wasn't here. He's looking for work at a wind farm." The trailer bucked. "Whoa." I grabbed the refrigerator handle.

"What was that?" Sheriff Marge asked.

"Hang on."

I poked my head into the bedroom. I couldn't see Jim. "Everything okay?"

He popped up on the far side of the bed. "Just checking if I could wedge the carpet under the bed frame." He frowned. "Can't."

"Meredith?" Sheriff Marge's voice sounded tinny coming from the phone in my hand.

I hurried outside and put the phone to my ear. "It's okay. Jim is here installing carpet. He, uh—well, he has bull-in-a-china-shop tendencies."

"Speaking of which, did you talk to him about unloading the semitrailer?"

"Briefly. I'll follow up."

"If Verle's unloading, I'll have him move the semi, too. Agent Simmons should be finished with it in another half hour or so."

"That's fast."

"That's 'cause Dale already collected anything worth calling evidence. I can safely say every shred of packing material and splintered wood and a couple cockroach legs are now in my storeroom."

I snorted.

"Tomorrow's your turn with them. Fair warning." Sheriff Marge clicked off.

I wrinkled my nose. What did she mean? Probably the list of questions I was supposed to memorize and then deliver to Earl in a casual manner. Yeah, right.

I hadn't told Sheriff Marge my worries about Ford. But that's all they were—worries. With no proof—no, I would never cast suspicion on Ford.

I stuffed the phone in my pocket and picked up a tarp corner. Dragging it off the picnic table, I smoothed it on the ground and began folding. Tuppence tried to help by standing in the middle.

"Get off, you silly dog. Go on." I waved my arms. "You're stinking up Jim's nice tarp." I giggled, then sighed.

One thing—maybe one thing in my life was getting back to normal. But the trailer lurched again, violently, making the door, which I'd left unlatched, swing open halfway before slamming shut. Muffled variations of several swear words spouted from my bedroom.

I placed the tarp and bungee cords in Jim's truck and collected the scattered tools into an empty five-gallon bucket. I perched on the picnic bench and tousled Tuppence's ears. "I think it'd be safer to stay out here for a while."

The hound snorted.

I inhaled sharply and pulled out my phone. Messages—I hadn't had a chance to check. There were a couple from Sally and one from Greg reporting on the wood-sample testing process. I dialed his number.

"Hey, did I catch you at a bad time?"

"Nope. I'm in the library, but nobody's around. So if I whisper it'll be okay," Greg said. "Would you like a reason to visit campus? Dr. Markey wants to use your wood sample to teach his class how to operate a new microscope. He said you're welcome to observe."

"There's been a glitch. They'll have to go ahead without me."

"Glitch?"

I couldn't tell him about the gold—not yet. The murder was turning into a convenient excuse. I cringed—how horrible to think of Ham as an excuse. "You've never met him, but you know about my ex-fiancé, right?"

There was a long silence on Greg's end. "Yeah."

"He came to visit—unexpectedly—and ended up murdered on the museum grounds Friday night."

Greg exhaled. "Tell me about you. Are you okay?"

I sniffed. Why did the tears spring up so fast? "Yes. I found him, though, and I'm a suspect because my phone was at the crime scene. It was stolen."

"Oh man. Meredith, I'm sorry. They'll have to clear you soon. How are you, really?"

"Confused. Sad. I'm not quite sure what to think."

"No kidding. I'm going to keep asking. You've always been there for me, so don't think you can get out of this."

I bit my lip. "Thanks," I whispered. "Can I change the subject?"

"Not yet. Are there any other leads? I don't like the idea of a murderer at large."

"Sheriff Marge is working on the case—I guess it just takes time. Lindsay's okay. She's not staying at the museum after dark." I took a breath. "Lindsay said you're writing a reference for her college application. I thought maybe—Wazzu is kind of far from OSU."

"You're forgetting her home and my internship are in the same town. We'll be seeing each other quite a lot on weekends." His smile was evident in his voice. "So now who's being nosy?"

"Just keeping tabs on you."

"The door swings both ways. If I'm forthcoming, I expect you to be, too."

"Fair enough."

"I'll be there Thursday night."

"Okay." I hung up and leaned forward, elbows on knees.

Sadness, gratitude—emotions swirled around. I'd pushed people away after Ham's betrayal, but now people were pushing back into my life. Relief—that's what the feeling was—relief. Arlene wanted to be my surrogate mom. Greg was already my surrogate brother. And Sheriff

Marge? She hovered, dropping in now and then like a what?—a surrogate fairy godmother.

I laughed at the image—a tiny pair of wings beating blurry double time to keep a tilted, Kevlar-vested Sheriff Marge a few inches off the ground. She pointed her stubby finger instead of a wand.

Then I realized Jim was standing before me, hands on hips.

"Done," he said.

I rose and followed him back into the trailer.

"Reglued the wallpaper, too," he said, pointing to the spots on both sides of the room where the wallpaper had partially slipped off the walls. "Unless you look real close, won't even know it was damaged."

"It's perfect." I removed my shoes and buried my toes in the thick carpet. "The color's nice. Sandstorm, huh? It'll hide everything. I won't have to vacuum more than once a month."

Jim grinned, his jowls broadening at chin level. He had nice, even teeth. The first time I'd seen him smile.

"I'll call Verle," he said.

"I'm going back to the museum now, too. So when you're ready—"

"Yep." He was already out the door.

ooo

I spent the next hour in my office, shoving books back on shelves. The arrangement was new, but not organized—there was no time for a thorough overhaul. The office needed to be presentable for the meeting with Earl. I borrowed the feather duster from Lindsay and swooshed it around, flinging a couple of years' worth of dust bunnies into the air. I sneezed.

I pushed the windows open as far as they would go. Maybe the perpetual gorge breeze would finish the task. I quickly scootched my loose papers into a pile and plunked a glass paperweight on top.

My phone rang.

"I'm turning the semi and trailer over to Verle, and Jim has him rigging a sling contraption to one of your crates. Thought you might want to supervise," Sheriff Marge said in a hoarse whisper.

"Be right there." I pulled on my coat and dashed downstairs.

I tossed the feather duster on the glass jewelry counter in the gift shop and thanked Lindsay, then trotted to the far end of the parking lot. I arrived, huffing and puffing, at the semi cab, where Sheriff Marge was filling out some paperwork. Too many grilled cheese sandwiches, not enough hiking.

"Doesn't T&T Trucking want their truck back?" I asked.

Sheriff Marge finished writing the VIN number in little boxes before replying. "We're towing it to Verle's lot for now—just to get it out of here. T&T's dispatcher said an insurance adjuster would come have a look at it tomorrow."

"What about the list Terry made—of the deliveries he's done for T&T? Anything suspicious?"

Sheriff Marge shrugged. "I gave the list to WSP. Most of the deliveries were up north. This was the only one in Sockeye County. The bow-tie guys in their commercial vehicle division will follow up."

"Bow-tie?"

"You haven't heard that before? Washington State Patrol—they're taller, better looking, and wear bow ties. I'm sure they can handle it."

A motor started. I knew the sound—a winch. It strained and groaned, then a horrible screech came from the trailer.

I ran to the trailer's back end.

"Steady—got it," Jim shouted from inside.

A young man, maybe midtwenties, with dark-blond, shoulder-length hair and a goatee, was operating a large tow truck's winch. Slowly one of my crates slid toward the edge of the trailer, then hung suspended under the tow truck's arm.

The young man switched off the winch and nodded at me. "Name's Verle. Where do you want them?"

I extended my hand, and Verle shook it. "Meredith. Nice to meet you. How about lined up at the edge of the parking lot, as close to that big tree"—I pointed—"as you can?"

Verle climbed in the cab and eased the tow truck across the long parking lot toward the museum, the crate rocking in its cradle behind. He reversed the winch to let the cable out, and set the crate gently on the pavement.

"Yep. He's as good as his daddy," Jim said, leaning against the trailer's rear doorframe.

After unhooking the harness, Verle returned to the semitrailer and backed into position for the next crate.

Sheriff Marge handed him the paperwork. "I'm going to pick up Terry and we'll be back soon. Thanks, Verle."

I hurried after Sheriff Marge and leaned into the Explorer's open window. "You're going to let Terry drive the truck?"

"Yep. The fifth-wheel connection is damaged from the jackknifing, so either Verle makes two trips or Terry drives the tractor while Verle tows the trailer. It's time to kick Terry out of jail anyway. He's getting on my nerves."

"You don't think he had anything to do with the shipment or the robbery?"

Sheriff Marge shrugged. "I'm not going to get any more out of him. Best to turn him loose but keep an eye out. If he was involved, he'll make a mistake and we'll catch him."

Forty-five minutes later, my statues sat in a neat row, and Verle was hooking the semitrailer to his tow truck.

I headed into the museum for peace and quiet and maybe a little work.

CHAPTER 15

I missed the sunset—and to have one at all is a rare occurrence in November when overcast cloud layers block the sun for days on end. I hunched over the keyboard, typing descriptions for a collection of animal windup toys from the 1920s. They were well built and still sturdy enough to survive what they were originally intended for—being played with by children. Maybe Mac could build a wooden racecourse for a hands-on display both kids and dads would enjoy.

My desk phone rang, and I felt for the receiver without looking and pulled it to my ear.

"Meredith?" Earl whispered.

I cringed. "Yes?"

"I was just thinking—I mean, is everything all right with my shipment? What size U-Haul do you think I should rent? I've been trying to estimate how big the crates are."

I dove toward the second question, hoping he would forget about the first. "The smallest truck should be fine."

"Not a trailer? We have a van with a hitch, so I could tow a small cargo trailer."

"Do you know the total weight and cubic dimensions of your shipment?" I held my breath and reached for Terry's paperwork. Why hadn't I thought to check that myself?

Earl fumbled the phone with several bumps. It sounded as if he was opening and closing drawers.

I found the numbers on the bill of lading and did some quick calculations. Gold weight, assuming eight statues per each of the fourteen crates, was in the neighborhood of 250 pounds. Crate weight plus the nominal wooden statue weight I estimated at 20 pounds per crate, or 280 pounds. The crate I'd opened was beefy—had to be, given its contents. A grand total of approximately 530 pounds. The bill of lading said 523. Reasonable.

"Here it is," Earl said. "Except I don't know how to read these things."

"About one-third of the way down the page," I replied. "There should be a row of boxes with numbers typed in them. Find the 'Net weight' box."

"Right. Two hundred and seventy-five. The weight's not a problem, then—that's the equivalent of two passengers. But the size—"

Ahh, a CPA—Earl could do fast calculations in his head, too.

"How big is your van? Can you take the backseats out?" I asked.

"That'd be best. If I rent a U-Haul, Mona will find out." Earl sighed. "For some reason I thought the shipment would be huge since it was coming through a trucking company. I expected big crates and lots of packing material."

"They combined shipments. Mine's the bulky one." I decided to take a shot in the dark. What motivated Earl? "Doesn't Mona appreciate art?"

"Not for its own sake. She likes art only if other people are impressed by it. She has no idea of its intrinsic value."

"Are you starting a gallery? Your secretary thought perhaps you were."

Earl's laugh was dry and brittle. "No, nothing like that. I'm working with a small group of like-minded aficionados. Entirely private, just personal interest—" His voice faded. "Well, thank you. I'll see you Wednesday." He hung up.

I reviewed my calculations. Why was Earl's paperwork different from Terry's? Or had he lied about the weight listed on his copy? The difference between the two was almost exactly my gold weight estimate.

There was something fishy in Earl's evasiveness about the private collectors. Why couldn't they be named? Were ugly wooden statues really so valuable that the new owners' identities needed to be protected? And the origin of the shipment in England—I should have asked about that.

I sighed. If these questions weren't on Eyebrows's and Superman's script, I might ad-lib a few of my own.

My phone rang—again.

"I'm about to leave, but Terry's here," Lindsay said. "And his mother. He wants to talk to you."

My eyebrows shot up. "Okay. Send them up. Hey, did you submit your application?"

"All done." Lindsay's grin could be heard in her voice.

"It's dark."

"My dad's picking me up tonight. You need to leave, too—soon."

"I'll walk out with Terry and his mom. We'll be fine."

I waited for the gentle hum of the elevator—if Terry's mom had emphysema, as he claimed, she wouldn't be climbing stairs. Why did I always wonder if what Terry said was true? And why wasn't I afraid of the at-large murderer the way Lindsay was? My brain seemed to have its fight-or-flight priorities mixed up.

A soft chime sounded, and I stepped into the hall to greet Terry and Mrs. Ambrose.

A scrawny woman leaned on Terry's arm. I accepted her feeble handshake, then continued holding her hand to guide her into the office and settle her on a folding chair. She perched like a featherless bird—hollow, plucked, weighing far too little even for her diminutive size. Mrs. Ambrose looked as though she might crumple to the floor in a pile of dust and calico print fabric.

She surrendered to a wheezy coughing fit, and pressed a flowered hankie to her mouth with a knobby hand. Terry held a water bottle at the ready.

Mrs. Ambrose's tightly permed hair retained a touch of the old-lady, beauty-salon lavender plus a tan tobacco tinge. She was the ideal candidate for an antismoking ad campaign—the kind that said, "Think cigarettes don't kill? Think again."

I pressed my lips together to prevent the thought from flying out.

Terry edged onto a chair next to his mother and watched anxiously until she resumed the rattle that seemed to be her normal breathing.

"Terry tells me you saved his life," Mrs. Ambrose croaked.

"Just helped. I don't think he was in mortal danger." I pressed my lips into a tight smile—nice things, I was supposed to be saying nice things to this very sick old woman. "I'm so pleased you've come to visit."

Mrs. Ambrose patted Terry's knee. "Terry wanted to say thank you and good-bye."

"So you drove down today?"

"Terry called to say he could come home, but without his truck—" Mrs. Ambrose hacked for a few seconds and looked at her son, apparently finished speaking.

"I needed a ride," Terry said. "And Mother's been worried." He nodded recognition of my frown. "I'm driving her back."

"I insisted," the old lady said. "I don't get out of the house much. And this is such a pretty part of the state. My first husband—Terry's father—and I came out here on our honeymoon, to Wenatchee."

I glanced at Terry. Wenatchee was several hours north in central Washington—beautiful, yes; nearby, no.

Terry took his mother's hand. "It'll be a late night. We should hit the road." He helped her stand, then shifted awkwardly, scanning my bookcase-lined walls. "Your delivery—statues, was it? Where are they?"

"You drove right by them—in the parking lot. They're still in their crates until—"

"Oh, yeah," Terry mumbled. "I heard. Sorry for your loss."

I escorted them downstairs and out through the main entrance. The parking lot was pitch-black except for a couple of buzzing halogen lights. No wonder Terry hadn't noticed the crates. I shivered.

"Will you let me know how things work out for you, with your employment and—" I hesitated.

"Parole." Terry nodded. "You've been kind. Thanks."

He eased Mrs. Ambrose into the front passenger seat of a late-1970s Chrysler New Yorker. The springs squeaked as she shifted her slight body on the cushioned bench. Terry gently latched the door.

He turned to me. "I know the sheriff still suspects me." He sighed. "Maybe you could put in a good word for me."

"I'd like to, but I don't—I don't really know you. I don't know what happened."

Terry glared for a brief second, then hung his head. "What I said—that's what happened. Nobody believes me."

"Terry, your record—"

"I know. I know." He waved me off and circled the New Yorker. He sank into the driver's seat and slid the big car with the quietly thrumming engine into the darkness. I watched his taillights turn left on State Route 14.

I hoped, for both their sakes, that Terry truly was innocent.

ooo

The next morning the feds were waiting for me in front of the museum. Eyebrows hopped out of the unmarked navy-blue van as I pulled into my parking spot.

"We'll need a small room adjacent to your office."

"Of course." I thought he meant an out-of-the-way place to drink coffee and work on their script. Maybe Sheriff Marge had kicked them out of the cramped modular building that housed the sheriff's deputies and dispatcher/office manager.

Then he yanked open the van's rear doors, revealing rolls of wire, electrical cords, and power tools. He pulled out a tray containing a drill, a hammer, screwdrivers, a laser measuring device, plus other items I didn't recognize.

"Wait a minute. What are you planning to do?"

"Wire your office for sound and a video feed."

I opened my mouth, but Eyebrows kept on talking. "Or you wear a recording and transmitting device, but hardwired's better, especially in that old building." He jerked his head toward the museum.

"That *old building* is on the National Register of Historic Places. Also, the interior walls are lath and plaster. No holes."

"Pinpricks. You'll never notice." Eyebrows rummaged in the van, his top half out of view and his voice muffled.

A door slammed and Superman put in an appearance. He'd been on a phone call in the driver's seat. "Morning, Ms. Morehouse."

I scowled. "No holes."

"Now, Ms. Morehouse, we'll use existing holes wherever we can—wiring, plumbing runs, and the like. The bookcases along the walls are an excellent place to hide a couple tiny cameras. And we clean up—all our equipment will be removed, and we'll patch any holes we had to make. Scout's honor." He held up three fingers pressed together.

I strode toward the Imogene's front doors, mulling a comeback. Suddenly my life was filled with a string of characters I didn't trust—Ham (a rerun), Terry, Earl, the fed boys. I wished for a magic wand that would—*poof!*—make them all disappear.

Never mind. I bit my tongue. Considering Ham's demise, my wish was cruel. Selfish—I was becoming selfish in my hermit-y old age.

Pinpricks, huh? Jim probably knew how to patch lath and plaster. He seemed to know how to do everything else. My outlook ought to be more pleasant today, considering I'd slept in my own bed last night for the first time in several days, thanks to Jim.

Focusing on grateful thoughts didn't help. I grumped up the stairs, Eyebrows and Superman on my heels.

The men perused the third floor and decided on the storage room where folding chairs, extra doors, a dress form, dusty lightbulb cartons, a pack of ant traps, and some miscellaneous mechanical equipment (maybe the innards of several defunct appliances?) were mishmashed together—all in the space of a standard closet.

"Where can we put all this stuff?" Superman asked.

"The basement. I'll show you." I grinned inwardly. I'd been meaning to clean out the storage room for years. If these fellows were going to drill holes in my walls, they could compensate with some heavy lifting.

A couple of hours later, amid the thumps and scritches coming from inside the walls as though a hundred laboratory mice were running mazes between the beams, Sheriff Marge stuck her head into my office.

"The boys are setting things up, I see."

I pointed to a growing pyramid of plaster dust on a shelf in the corner. "A wire keeps poking through that hole, then disappearing again. In—out, in—out. Like a mole shoving dirt from its tunnel." I clenched my hands into fists, fingernails making half-moon indentations in my palms. "I'm going crazy."

"Let's walk," Sheriff Marge said.

I quickly followed her already-retreating broad backside. To the best of my knowledge, Sheriff Marge did not partake of exercise—chasing bad guys being more than enough to meet her exertion quota. But she sure could hustle. I trotted to catch up.

Outside, Sheriff Marge squeezed between two statue crates and aimed directly for the trench.

"Um." I slowed.

Sheriff Marge pulled a small Swiss Army knife from her pocket and sliced through the crime scene tape. "Help me with this." She walked the perimeter, balling the tape in her hands.

I picked up the free end and worked counterclockwise, releasing the tape from tree limbs and wooden stakes in the ground. I met Sheriff Marge on the opposite side.

"So you're finished with the scene." I knew the answer but said it anyway.

Mesmerized, I stared into the trench. The bottom was covered with footprints and depressions—where Ham had lain, where the medical tech had knelt beside him, where Sheriff Marge and her deputies had squatted to examine things from a different angle. It was a churned mess of merged divots. Then the image of his face flashed on the screen in my mind.

I jerked my eyes away, turned to Sheriff Marge. "Do you know who did it yet?"

"Not for sure, but I've bumped a suspect to the top of my list."

"Who?"

"Ferris. Or whatever his name is."

I squinted. "What motive?"

"Don't know, but he sure disappeared in a hurry. I've talked to all the wind-farm managers in a hundred-mile radius. None of them saw a man matching his description. They all said they hire through their companies' HR departments. They'd never hire someone who just showed up looking for work."

"But he left things at his campsite."

"Lucky for us. Dale dusted for prints and is running them through the system."

"An outsider."

"That'd make me feel better, if it's the case." Sheriff Marge pursed her lips.

"But known to Ham. The look on his face—he knew his killer." I grabbed Sheriff Marge's arm. "Arlene won't see that, will she? Don't let her—"

"No. The muscles relax, you know—rigor mortis fades. She's prepared for a closed casket. I told her that's the norm after an autopsy."

"He was kind of jumpy," I said.

"Who?"

"Ferris. When I introduced myself at the campground. And I sort of thought he was following me a day or two before that—on the way to the hospital in Lupine."

"Why didn't you tell me before?" Sheriff Marge glowered over her reading glasses.

I shrugged. "He seemed nice at the Sidetrack. I just thought he was uncomfortable around strangers. I get that way myself."

"He sat next to you at the bar, right?"

"I sat next to him. He was already there." I frowned. "You don't think—my phone?"

"Yes, I do."

"Why?"

"I'll have to figure that out. And find him."

"Could have been a museum visitor. Lindsay said two guys came in together, spent a lot of time looking around. Maybe they were picking up anything not nailed down."

"Notice anything else missing?"

"Not yet."

"Yoo-hoo." Superman was picking his way across the wet grass, apparently concerned about the moisture's effect on his wing tips.

I wrinkled my nose. Had he actually just yoo-hooed? I kicked at a dirt clod so he wouldn't see my grin.

"We're set," he said, huffing slightly. "We need to test the equipment and go over the script."

Sheriff Marge wedged the ball of caution tape under her arm and marched after him. I took up the rear.

The boys had made good on their promise to clean up. I scanned the bookshelves, where everything was back in place. A couple of titles were tipped at different angles from before, making the scant openings needed for the cameras. I stepped to the corner shelf and peered between two books.

"Uh, really, Ms. Morehouse, there's no need—" Superman jumped forward and grabbed my outstretched hand. "Don't touch it. They're aimed perfectly."

"Now, if you two will have a seat"—Eyebrows pulled a folding chair out for Sheriff Marge—"and have a conversation at normal volume, I'll check the mikes."

The men hurried from the office. Sheriff Marge and I looked at each other.

Sheriff Marge cleared her throat. "So how was Thanksgiving with Pete?"

"You're asking me *now*?" I hissed.

Sheriff Marge shrugged. "Been kind of busy."

"Fine. It was fine."

"I've never been on his tug. It's quite an honor he invited you."

"The Levines were there, too."

Sheriff Marge tapped her foot. Then she thrummed her fingers on her knee. "Got a new microwave."

"Oh. That's nice."

"Old one died."

"Tuppence is smelling better."

Sheriff Marge nodded sagely. "Takes a while."

I shuffled papers. "Did I tell you the color of my new carpet is 'Sandstorm'?"

"Brown?" Sheriff Marge squinted.

"Goes with everything."

"Sure has been wet lately."

"It's always wet in November."

"Yep."

We both glanced at the open doorway.

I rearranged the piles on my desk. "Met Terry's mother yesterday."

"Me, too. Thought I was going to have to call an ambulance for her."

Superman popped into the room. "We're good. Now for the script." He handed me a couple of sheets of paper.

I quickly scanned the pages. They wanted dates, times, names—just the facts. "Do I have to memorize these?"

"You need to be very familiar with them—comfortable, but not rote. We don't want to make Mr. Rittenour suspicious."

Great. I inhaled. "He's already highly strung. But I don't think he knows about the gold. His worries about the shipment have always been about the wood statues—whether they're safe from moisture, the elements." I frowned. "His secretary said he already owns a few statues, but his comments indicated this is his first time handling a shipment. Is it possible there are two things going on? Some kind of double cross?"

Sheriff Marge leaned in. "You boys have any ideas about who stole the majority of the shipment?"

Eyebrows shrugged. "The trailer was super clean. We think they opened only a crate or two to verify the contents, then took the rest intact."

"Were they after the gold or the statues or both?" I asked.

"I think it's safe to say the gold is the more valuable of the two," Eyebrows said. "My team hasn't identified the statues yet. Nothing's matched up with reported-stolens from any museums or private collections. We're not sure of their origin. They might be fake. But if that's the case, what are they meant to be forgeries of?"

I sighed. I could have told him all that. "Whatever it takes to fool Mr. Rittenour. Have you checked his travel history? Has he been to Africa, Australia, or anywhere else, for that matter, in the past few years?"

Both Superman and Eyebrows were scowling at me.

"Wouldn't it be a good idea to know if he bought the statues he already owns directly or through a dealer—what kind of contacts he has in the art world, if any?" They were still staring. "At least, that's something I'd like to know," I muttered.

"Good idea." Sheriff Marge stood and used her bulk to usher the men toward the door.

Superman turned at the threshold. "Tomorrow we'll find out how gullible Mr. Rittenour is. Or if he knows something we don't." He pointed at me. "That's your job."

A few seconds later, Sheriff Marge ducked back into my office. "We forgot to share that tidbit with them earlier—about Rittenour already owning statues." She grinned. "They'll get over it."

I slumped in my chair and exhaled. With so many pieces of information swirling around in my head, and having to keep track of what I could say to whom—better to err on the side of sharing too little information than too much. Still, I'd be angry if I'd been left in the dark. Maybe they were pulling a snow job. How could they have no idea who'd stolen the shipment?

I chuckled. Did certain species of cockroaches hail from certain regions? Maybe Dale's son could find the answer faster than the feds.

CHAPTER 16

I spent the next hour trying to massage the feds' questions into my brain. I scrawled several acrostics in the margins, then regrouped the questions into different themes. I rubbed my forehead. Maybe if the conversation flowed naturally, most of the questions would be answered in due course.

If Earl wasn't too skittish, we could easily have a lot to talk about. Maybe I'd give him a tour of the Imogene—wouldn't Superman and Eyebrows love that?

My brain was full. I folded the pages and stuffed them in my tote for review later. The windup toys beckoned, and I opened their photos-and-descriptions document on my laptop.

"Hey there."

I whirled around. Pete—*clean-shaven*, sparkly-blue-eyed, hunky Pete. My mouth fell open. He had ruddy skin where the stubble had been, and a square chin. I might just faint from hormones.

"Finished the job sooner than expected. But I have another one starting tomorrow, so I can't come over this weekend." He inhaled. "How about an early dinner?"

"Now?" My mind flashed over my pantry shelves—bare. I'd left one crust in the bread bag this morning—couldn't even make grilled cheese sandwiches. "Um—"

Oh, but he looked good. He needed a haircut—it was getting a little shaggy at the edges. I could run my fingers through—there, at the back of his neck. Was I supposed to be saying something?

"I packed a picnic."

"Okay." I realized I had a silly smile plastered on my face.

"I got something else, too." Pete's grin mirrored mine.

My eyebrows shot up.

Pete tipped his head toward the hallway, beckoning.

I closed the laptop, stuffed my phone in my coat pocket, and followed him downstairs. I waved to Lindsay in the gift shop, and she replied with a very soft catcall whistle, pointing at Pete's back as he pushed open the glass front doors.

I quickly checked that he hadn't heard and ducked into the gift shop. "Shh!"

Lindsay shook her head and grinned. "You two behave, now."

I scowled.

"Quick—go," Lindsay said. "I think he wants to show you something." She winked. "I already peeked." She flapped both hands, urging me out.

I hurried to the front doors. Pete stood next to a low-slung motorcycle—spotless black paint and chrome pipes, black leather saddlebags draped over the rear wheel, begging for the open road and clear skies. He held two helmets by their straps.

"The guy I did this last job for is struggling financially. He offered the bike as partial payment." If anything, Pete's smile was broader now. "It's a little small for me—but it fits on the tug, which is the main thing." He pointed at the second leather seat over the back fender. "And there's room for a passenger."

I inhaled. "Wow." My fingertips and something in the vicinity of my appendix tingled. It couldn't be worse than a roller coaster.

I'd thrown up in the middle and at the end of my last roller-coaster ride, when I was nine. The people seated in the row behind hadn't appreciated it. At least I'd be on the tail end of the motorcycle—with a helmet over my head.

I ground my molars. "Great." I would not be a ninny in front of—or behind—Pete.

Pete's smile faded. "Have you ridden a motorcycle before?"

"Nope."

"Just hang on—to me." The grin was back.

He was going to be black and blue from my hanging on. No way to hide that. I reached for a helmet and crammed it on my head.

Pete flipped my face mask up. "I'll get on first and start the bike," he shouted. "Then you get on. Watch out for the exhaust pipe—it gets hot." He cinched the strap under my chin. "When we go around corners or curves, lean into them, okay? Wrap your arms around me and follow what I do."

I nodded my giant noggin.

The motorcycle started with a rackety roar and settled into a deep growl. My helmet muffled the noise down to lawn-mower decibels. Pete stretched out a hand, and I grabbed it. I swung my leg over and slid onto the padded square that was to be my berth.

Pete grabbed my calf and lifted my leg. My eyes about popped out before I realized he was placing my foot on a short peg—a footrest. I found the peg on the other side by myself.

I tentatively rested my hands against Pete's sides.

"Here we go," Pete yelled over his shoulder, and smacked his face mask closed.

I reached up to close my face mask, and the bike lurched forward. With a squeal I flung my arms around Pete. The snaps on the front of his jacket were cool under my palms.

We couldn't have been going very fast, but with the air rushing by—tugging at my pant legs and sleeves, pummeling my helmet—it felt as though we were flying.

At the end of the parking lot, Pete leaned onto the access road, and my stomach nearly had an out-of-body experience. I squeezed my eyes shut and pressed my face mask between Pete's shoulder blades. He'd said to lean with him, so I did—and focused on his strong, broad back instead of how close my knee was to the pavement.

It was over in a second, and Pete accelerated toward the highway. I thought maybe he needed space to breathe and relaxed my grip a little.

Out on the straight highway, when the imminent danger of falling off had passed, I eased back, still clutching handfuls of rough buffalo plaid wool. Tucked in behind Pete, I found the wind wasn't too bad, and I had a glorious, unobstructed view of the Columbia River Gorge.

Giant cloud poufs, like escaped pillow stuffing, dotted the sky and cast shadows over brown rolling hills tinged with green. The river was deep blue with a few whitecaps, and flowing high and silent from the recent rain.

A semi passed, going in the opposite direction, blasting us with its wake. I renewed my vise grip. My hands were freezing.

We passed a westbound train with four orange BNSF—Burlington Northern Santa Fe— engines straining at the harness. Coal, scrap metal, wheat hoppers, oil tank cars, and intermodal containers blurred into a mile-long streak.

Pete slowed and pulled off the highway into a small state park. At the end of November, we had the place to ourselves. He coasted the bike to the edge of the river, and I slid off. My backside was numb, and I was suddenly warm inside my jacket.

Pete set the bike on the kickstand. "Well?"

"Exhilarating. Wow." I ran my fingers through my hair, trying to undo the flattening effects of the helmet.

Pete pulled a blanket, thermoses, and wrapped packages out of the saddlebags. "It'll be dark soon, so if you want to see what you're eating—" He kicked a few rocks and pinecones out of the way and spread the blanket on the leeward side of a boulder outcropping.

I dropped to my knees and finished the spreading. "What'd you bring?"

"Turkey soup." Pete grimaced. "Not fancy, but it's what I had."

I chuckled.

"And a couple of cheese-and-tomato sandwiches, because I'm a classy guy." He grinned.

"Hey. That's the epitome of gourmet in my book. Don't knock it." I reached for a thermos.

Pete settled beside me—right beside me. Our shoulders bumped. I poured a mug of soup and handed it to him, then poured one for myself. We slurped. I pulled my knees up and wrapped my arms around them.

"Cold?"

"The soup helps. What'd you put in it?"

"Everything left over except the pie. Why?"

"I just got a chunk of yam."

Lights winked on a channel navigation marker on the Oregon side. It was so peaceful and calm—not much breeze. The water lapped against the rocky shore—midnight blue now, an inky ribbon.

I inhaled. "I love it here."

"The river's really gotten under your skin, hasn't it? You were all skittery when you first came. The river's a calming influence."

"Skittery?" I pulled away and scowled.

"Jumpy. Tense. Didn't take time to appreciate beauty—or people." He leaned over and pulled me back, his arm around my waist.

"I was working on getting over—well, I had a good reason. Oh—" I straightened and turned again toward Pete. "You probably don't know, since you just got back." My stomach knotted.

His eyebrows—two dark lines in the deepening shadow—drew together. His eyes looked black.

I exhaled. "Ham, my ex-fiancé—you met him at Junction General—was murdered Friday night on the museum grounds. My cell phone was found under his body, so I'm a suspect."

Pete's lips pressed together in a tight line, easier to see without the stubble. "Meredith—" He reached for me, but I rocked to my haunches and stood.

"I'm sorry. I should have told you sooner."

"Wait—hold on." Pete scrambled to his feet. "How are you?" He shook his head. "Why didn't you?"

I shrugged. "I wanted to. Sheriff Marge had my phone because it's evidence. And I didn't get a replacement until yesterday. After that, well—"

Pete stuffed his hands in his pockets.

"I'm really sorry. It's not fair to you—I'm sorry." I stooped and collected thermoses and wrappers.

Pete was still staring at me. What did he think of me now?

"Will you take me back, please?" I turned away to hide my tears.

My phone rang. I set everything down again and fished in my pocket.

"Hello?" I tried to make my shaky voice sound normal.

"Meredith, you okay?" Greg asked.

"Yeah."

"Um, okay. Got the microscopic wood-analysis results. Disappointing, though."

"What do you mean?"

"Western hemlock."

"I'm not following."

"I thought you were hoping for an exotic wood, and you mentioned the wood was heavy or dense, but it isn't particularly. Just ordinary hemlock, which is native to this area—the Pacific Northwest coastal range."

"Oh." I placed a hand on a boulder to steady myself. "Doesn't it grow anywhere else?"

"It was introduced to northern Europe, Britain, and southern New Zealand for timber and paper production."

"Okay." I released a shuddery sigh. "Thank you for arranging the analysis, for going out of your way."

"You know I love research. What's wrong? Is it to do with Ham's murder?"

"Can I call you back? Please, Greg—later?"

"You promise?"

"Yeah."

Pete was in the same spot—still standing on the blanket, still staring at me. I bent to scoop up the picnic trappings again so he couldn't see my face—probably a white smudge in the darkness. Would it be awful to let him see me cry? What had I done? Showed him I didn't trust him, didn't think of him, maybe betrayed his trust in me.

I rose to face him, opened my mouth to repeat my apology. But before the words came out my phone rang again. Pete stepped forward and took the thermos from my hands.

"Hello?"

"The prints came back," Sheriff Marge said. "Several aliases, but his real name's Edward Fulmer."

"Criminal history?" I leaned against the boulder and fixed my gaze on the pulsing navigation light.

"A mile long, but never convicted in Washington. Served time in California, Montana, and Nevada."

"Do you know where he is?"

"Nope. Put out a BOLO."

"A what?"

"Be on the lookout."

"You think he's the one?"

"My gut says yes, but no evidence yet."

"So I'm not off the hook."

"Unfortunately, no."

"Thanks for telling me."

Pete had everything packed in the saddlebags and his helmet on. He handed me the second helmet. He fired up the bike, and I climbed on—no fear, no nervous anticipation, no exhilaration this time. No thought about the danger. A motorcycle wreck would be inconsequential compared to what I'd just done to Pete.

A sprinkling of stars peeked between the dark, patchy clouds. My teeth chattered, and a few tears soaked into the helmet's padded lining. I'm terrible at communicating. Of course, Pete wouldn't want to date a murder suspect or be involved with someone whose past was as messy as mine. I'd presumed upon him without considering his feelings. It was all my stupid fault.

I wanted to rest my head on Pete's back and have a good old cry, but he probably wouldn't appreciate my hugging him right now. I blinked to get rid of the tears. Think about something else.

So Ferris was Edward Fulmer. He'd picked another *F* name—similar, easy to remember. Wait—Fulmer. Ozzie Fulmer, the cop-killer—the worst, or best, of Ham's trials, depending on which side you were on. The article I'd read listed Fulmer's relatives who'd sat in the courtroom throughout the entire trial, even included an interview with his mother. Was there an Edward on that list, or was Ferris's real name merely coincidence?

I flipped my face mask up and pounded on Pete's shoulder. When he turned his head and flipped his mask up, I yelled, "Can you go faster? I need to get to the museum right away."

Pete snapped his mask closed and gunned the bike. He hunched into the wind, and I ducked lower, pulled my knees in, and held on.

CHAPTER 17

The Imogene rose like a huge black box in the night. The exterior lighting did nothing to reveal the building's true dimensions or appearance. I slid off the motorcycle and fumbled with the helmet strap.

Pete killed the engine and removed his helmet first. "What's wrong?"

"Aarghh." My voice was muffled inside the helmet.

Pete pushed my hands away and unclipped the strap. He lifted the helmet straight up, and my hair popped out in a clown wig impersonation. I wrapped my arms over my head.

"I need to check something online. The last names match." I spun and trotted for the museum's front doors. I unlocked them and pushed through, Pete on my heels.

"Are you going to turn on the lights?" Pete asked as he tripped on the bottom riser of the grand staircase. The dim after-hours lighting was only in the ballroom and did nothing for the rest of the cavernous museum.

I was halfway up the staircase. "Sorry. I know my way around, so I didn't think—" I returned and grabbed his arm. "Here—with me. Step. Step. Got it?"

Pete muttered something unintelligible, and I dashed ahead.

On the landing I froze. The Imogene makes noises, like any old building—creaks and groans, ticks and clicks, air whooshing as the heating and cooling systems turn on and off. But this was different. The noise had stopped just before I did—in response to my movements.

And it wasn't Pete. He was still carefully thud-thud-thudding up the stairs in the dark—his boots heavy on the oak boards.

I turned to shush Pete, and my hand brushed something rough and fuzzy. I gasped, then realized it was Pete's jacket. His warm breath flitted across my face.

"Wha—" he began.

I flashed my hand toward his face, bumped his nose, and settled over his mouth.

"Mmmrf."

I clamped tighter and shook my head, hoping he could sense the movement. I felt around and tugged on his earlobe with my other hand. I held my breath, and Pete seemed to be doing the same.

His hand closed on my wrist, and he pulled my hand from his mouth. His other arm went around my waist. I squeezed my eyes shut, tipped my forehead against his chest, and concentrated on listening.

Seconds passed—minutes. The only thing I could hear was Pete's calm breathing, in time with the rise and fall of his chest.

A sharp crack—the parquet ballroom floor adjusting to the cooler after-hours temperature.

Clank, clank, clank—the radiator in the public restroom on the main floor.

Whooshiwooh, click, click—the furnace cycling on.

Shuffle—my eyes flew open and I stiffened.

Pete pressed his hand into the small of my back.

Shuffle. Shuffle.

Creeeak—the loose board on the fifteenth step up, the third step down, on the staircase between the second and third floors.

Long pause. Shuffle.

Someone was stealthily climbing to the third floor.

The third floor. My office. Where a prowler would start looking for the gold.

I pushed away from Pete. "I gotta go," I half whispered, half breathed, and kicked off my shoes.

I flew down the hall toward the servant's stairwell, slid past it on my wool socks, flailed backward, and fell through the swinging door. Just a bump—not too loud. I shot to my feet and dashed up the back stairs.

At the third-floor landing, I paused, panting, behind the swinging door. I wedged a fingertip in the gap and pulled the door toward me, opening a small crack to peek through. All black.

There. There again—short flashes of dim light arced under my office door at the far end of the hall. Someone was already inside.

My eyes adjusted to the darkness. I picked out shadows of doorways and the pedestal stand holding a bust of Rupert's great-great-uncle.

I'd pulled the swinging door open far enough to slide through when another dark shadow made me freeze. This one moved. A man's form (what woman would creep around a museum in the dark?) slunk to my office door, reached for the knob, seemed to be listening.

Warm air on my neck. My body went rigid and my hair stood on end.

"I'm coming with you," Pete whispered. He squeezed my arm. "I texted Sheriff Marge."

I hadn't heard him come up—I'd been so focused on the man in the corridor. Pete must have taken his boots off.

"I don't know how many." I pointed toward my office. Pete shifted for a better view.

The man listening at my office door turned the knob—I knew that faint squeal. It needed a good dose of 3-in-One Oil—and pushed into the room.

Grunts, hoarse yells, thuds, a crash. The flashlight beams became frantic.

"My laptop," I hissed.

I bolted down the hall, swiped the bust of Rupert's great-great-uncle on the way, and slid to a stop just in front of my office. I felt around the doorframe for the light switch, took a deep breath, and flipped it on.

Three men in the midst of grappling with one another blinked at me. A bookcase lay on its side, books strewn everywhere. It was the bookcase that had held the carefully positioned camera. Wires dangled from a gaping hole in the wall.

"You—" I screeched. "Lath and plaster!"

I flung the bust at the nearest man—Ferris, of all people, Ferris—but he ducked. He lunged, grabbed my legs, and pulled.

I fell hard against the file cabinet and slumped between the cabinet and a bookcase. Air whooshed from my lungs as though from a punctured balloon. I gasped and kicked my legs free. My injured shoulder, so recently released from the sling, throbbed.

"That's it." Ferris's voice cut like steel cable.

I gazed up at him, everything blurry about the edges, but he wasn't looking at me. He was pointing a gun at the doorway. I strained forward to see—Pete.

I'd entangled him in my emotional mess. Now he was also in mortal danger because of me. He probably wished he'd never met me.

Something happened to my vision. It narrowed to a point, as though I were staring through a tunnel at a bull's-eye. Ferris was the bull's-eye. Had he killed Ham? And now he had the gall to point a gun at my Pete. He was going down.

I scooted one foot underneath my body and launched up and out of the corner. Ferris had time only for a startled glance in my direction. He stumbled backward and fell across one of the other men. I landed on top of them—thrashing, jabbing for the gun. Where had it gone?

"Murderer," I grunted, wrestling with several pairs of arms and legs.

Ferris barked a short laugh. Half on top, he pinned my arms to my sides. "Had it coming, that pig."

He moved fast—so fast. I kicked and squirmed. My heel connected with something squishy. The man on the bottom of the pile shouted an obscenity. A short flash of space, and I bent my elbow between them and grabbed a handful of Ferris's ear and hair.

"Ham didn't deserve revenge. Ozzie's guilty," I wheezed, digging my fingernails into cartilage.

Ferris grunted. "Ozzie? Think what you want, but that pig made plenty of enemies," he spit out. "Should've seen his face. Coward."

Pete stood Ferris up, grasping him by the scruff of his neck. Then an arm in red-and-black buffalo plaid shot out straight and fast and collided with Ferris's jaw. Ferris buckled—just folded accordion-style into a pile on the floor without a sound.

I gaped, my brain trying to catch up with what my eyes had seen. Then the lump I was sitting on moved.

"Impressive," said a voice from the corner by the window.

A young man—he could have passed for a college student—with short brown hair and brown eyes slowly squatted and snagged a pistol—Ferris's pistol—from under the desk with his free hand. Now he had a gun in each hand. He trained them on Pete—arms extended, elbows locked. He meant business.

He nudged the man underneath me with his sneaker. "Get up, you idiot."

The man rolled over, upending me, and scrambled to his feet. He pulled a gun out of his back waistband and shakily aimed it at me.

"Not her, idiot. Him." The first man jerked his head toward Pete, then Ferris. "And him, in case he comes to. She's coming with me." He handed the extra gun to the second man.

He grabbed me by the hair and yanked me up. "I think you know what we're here for. And you're going to show me where it is."

He was inches from my face, and I fixated on his overlapped front teeth. Was this the man who'd flirted with Lindsay, who'd cased the museum?

From the look of things, they'd already searched my office and realized the gold wasn't in the room. How long until Sheriff Marge would arrive? Stall—I had to stall.

Pete, with his hands in the air, winked once rapidly—more like a flinch or a tic. What was he trying to tell me? I wrinkled my nose, tipped my head. What?

Snaggletooth waved Pete into the corner with his gun hand, and his buddy took up a rigid stance, legs spread, both guns pointed at Pete's stomach.

Snaggletooth's hand clamped on my sore shoulder, fingers clawing into the muscle, and he pushed me toward the door. "Let's go, sweetheart."

Conversation. Maybe he could be distracted. "Why did you scout the museum a couple days ago if you were just going to ransack it anyway?"

He jabbed the gun barrel into my side, and I yelped.

"Shut up and hurry up." He kneed me in the back of the thigh. "Or we'll torch the place, too."

My breath came in shallow gasps. *Think. Think. Don't make him any angrier—at least not until you have to.*

I walked stiff-legged, the gun prying into a gap between my ribs. I clenched my teeth against the pain.

Angling toward the dark hall instead of the stairs, I made each step take as long as possible. I wanted to be noisy, to clomp so everyone could hear my path, but with stockinged feet all I managed were light thumps. Was Sheriff Marge downstairs, listening, before mounting a charge?

Snaggletooth wrenched my shoulder back. "Tell me where we're going, or I'll have Mike blow your boyfriend's brains out," he hissed.

I sucked in a breath. Mike—the idiot—had appeared a little shaky, but at such short range he wouldn't miss. "End of the hall—servants' quarters. Tote bag in the laundry chute."

Snaggletooth shoved me forward. I stared into the darkness, my eyes dry and scratchy. If I couldn't see anything, he couldn't, either. Adrenaline buzzed through my veins as an idea formed.

Close to the staircase Pete and I had climbed, I ran my hand along the wall, searching for the latch to the laundry-chute hatch. My thumb just nicked the edge. "Here."

Snaggletooth pulled me back, found the latch, and opened the panel. "You do it." He pushed me toward the blacker black of the deep hole.

I grabbed the edge, about waist-high, and leaned forward, stretching my arm into the opening. My hand brushed against knobs and over empty toeholds on the chute's perimeter. Snaggletooth's raspy breathing echoed in the chamber as he pressed against me.

There. My fingers slid over the tote bag's strap resting on the top of a knob. I kept stretching, reaching lower, not wanting Snaggletooth to sense hesitation. Then I straightened quickly, bumping his nose with the back of my head.

But not hard enough. He jerked back and twisted the gun barrel into my side. I bit my lip to keep from crying out.

"Where is it?" His hot breath came in bursts against my cheek.

"I can't reach far enough. It's on the left, hanging from a knob."

"Sit." He shoved me to the floor. "Against the wall."

I scooted around his legs until I leaned against the wall just to his right.

"Don't move." He tapped the gun on my skull.

I flinched. *Focus*. I forced a deep, slow inhalation. Exhalation. Compared to the laundry chute, the corridor was bright—Snaggletooth stood out in sharp relief against the white wall.

He knocked me on the head with the gun one more time and leaned into the opening.

My head pounding, I bunched my leg muscles and slowly eased into a squat. I crab-walked a couple of feet and turned, directly behind Snaggletooth. He leaned farther. Timing would be everything.

I planted my feet, praying my socks would provide enough traction, and lightly fingered the hem of Snaggletooth's jeans.

His back disappeared—he was hinged over the edge of the opening at the waist.

"Got it." His voice was muffled.

I scooped my hands inside his pant legs, grabbed his skinny ankles, and stood, pulling his legs up—just high enough. He tipped over the edge and gravity took care of the rest. His scream reverberated inside the chute and trailed off.

A tremendous crash from the direction of my office shook the whole third floor.

I slammed the laundry-chute panel closed and ran.

"Missus Morehouse," Ford shouted from the top of the main stairs. I almost collided with him.

"Missus Morehouse." He was panting. "There's burglars."

"I know, Ford," I gasped, still sliding toward my office.

I sprawled over a chair that was lying in the doorway and tumbled to a stop on a firm body. Ferris—still out.

Three more bookcases had fallen, creating a mound of books—some spread open with pages wavering in an unfelt breeze, others in teetering stacks where they'd landed on each other. I scanned them quickly, looking for—there. Red-and-black buffalo plaid. Which was moving.

I tackled the pile, flinging books out of the way.

Ford dove in beside me. "What're you lookin' for?"

"Pete."

Muttering came from under the pile. Then a sharp shift in the mound, and Pete rose—books toppling—with two pistols in his hands.

He stared at me, chest heaving.

Then he gently set the guns on the desk, never taking his eyes off me. "I thought it was you. The scream—"

I shook my head for a long time before the words would come out. "Not me."

Ford scratched behind his ear. "There's burglars."

Pete stepped over the book avalanche, took my hand, and pulled me to my feet. "Not you."

Ferris groaned.

"This one of 'em?" Ford asked.

"Yeah. Will you keep an eye on him? There's another one under the bookcase." Pete captured my other hand.

Ford deftly pulled the bullet magazines from both pistols and dropped them into his coveralls pocket. He righted the chair, then hauled Ferris up and sat him in it. He pulled a couple of lengths of jute rope from another pocket and tied Ferris's wrists to the chair arms.

Pete rubbed circles on the backs of my hands with his thumbs. I forgot about everything except his sapphire-blue eyes and smooth cheeks and chin.

Ford fished Mike out from under the bookcase, then plunked him on the floor next to it and tied his wrists to different shelves.

"Anybody else?" Ford asked.

"Yeah. Me," said a voice from the doorway.

CHAPTER 18

Pete spun and stepped in front of me, making a kind of corral with his arms. Once again I was tucked behind his back. I peeked around his shoulder.

Snaggletooth, with blood running down the side of his face from a gash above his left eye, had the tote bag slung across his body. His gun hand was steady.

"B-but—you—" I stuttered.

"Had a nice, soft landing in a laundry cart. The big ones have springs, you know." Snaggletooth sneered. "Think you're clever, huh? Piece of cake. I'm a certified rock-climbing instructor."

He took a step into the room and gestured with the gun. "Come on, sugar. I'm not playing. Take me to the gold or someone dies." He swung the gun toward Ford's legs and fired before anyone could blink.

"No!" I shouted, but my voice was lost in the blast.

Ford jigged—too little, too late—and sagged against the file cabinet, his face contorted in pain.

Ears still ringing, I pushed forward. But Pete was moving, too, and I stumbled across the back of his legs.

Pete head-butted Snaggletooth before he had a chance to re-aim the pistol, and they crashed to the floor.

I scrabbled over them and grabbed Ford around the middle. I tried to help ease him to the floor, but he pushed up to standing.

"Ford, sit. It'll be better—stop the bleeding."

"Jes' winged me," Ford grunted.

"What?"

"Got my steel-toed boots on."

A khaki-colored blur joined the fray on the floor, and the pile of bodies rolled against the desk legs.

"You sure?" I backed Ford into the corner so he could hang on to the two remaining bookcases.

A second khaki form charged into the room—this one much bulkier and more imposing, though shorter.

"Got it, Dale?" Sheriff Marge asked.

"Yep." Dale's voice was muffled from his bending over. He grunted and clicked—a metal ratchet sound. "That's it. Thanks, Pete." Another click. Dale straightened.

Snaggletooth lay on his stomach, handcuffed and still, his face turned away from us.

Pete rose, another gun in his hand. He set it carefully on the desk by the other two. He blew out a deep breath, quickly scanned the people in the room, and found me. His eyes locked on.

No time for falling apart.

I knelt to examine Ford's feet. A channel cut through the leather of his right boot, starting at the outside edge of his toes and down the side for a couple of inches, just above the thick sole. I ran my pinkie fingertip in the channel and felt hard metal inside. There was a divot and grooved tail in the steel. But no hole.

I rose and wrapped an arm around Ford. "Ford needs medical attention. Bruises for sure, maybe broken toes. What took you so long?"

Sheriff Marge checked her watch. "Eighteen minutes." She cocked an eyebrow at me. "Do you know how big this county is?"

Heavy boots thundered up the stairs, and Archie rushed into the room, one hand clutching his waistband—or maybe his gun belt. It was hard to tell.

"Shucks. Did I miss the fun?"

Dale grinned. "Yep."

"But you can take Ford down to the ambulance," Sheriff Marge said.

"Use the elevator," I called as Ford limped away with his hand on Archie's shoulder for support.

"Well, well, well," Sheriff Marge said, taking in the three restrained men. "Mm-hmm." She stepped in front of Ferris and bent to peer at him over the tops of her reading glasses.

He glared back sullenly.

"Would you care to make a statement?"

"I was set up." He spit out the words.

"Mmm." She moved on to Mike, still affixed to the fallen bookcase. "And you are?"

"Mike—Michael Burton." His eyes shifted from side to side, then settled on the spot of bare floor between his knees.

Dale scrawled quickly in a small notebook.

"And you?" Sheriff Marge squatted beside Snaggletooth.

His body stiffened, and he refused to turn his head toward her.

"I see." Sheriff Marge rose. "You're all under arrest—attempted burglary, assault, suspicion of murder—" She pointed at Ferris. "There will be more charges, but that's enough of a list for now. Dale?"

"Yep." Dale snapped his notebook shut. "Hobart'll be here in a few minutes. We'll book 'em."

"I need the tote bag and its contents back," I said. "By tomorrow morning, anyway." Enough time for a quick glue job if the statues had been smashed, maybe. Images of toothpick-size smithereens flitted through my mind.

Sheriff Marge tipped her head, opened her mouth, closed it, and nodded. "Dale, leave the bag here in Meredith's office. You two"—she indicated Pete and me—"come with me."

We opted for the bright lights and gleaming white surfaces of the staff kitchen. I measured grounds and poured water into the coffeemaker. Pete scooted a few folding chairs around the table.

"I take it you two were together for the entire episode?" Sheriff Marge asked.

Pete nodded.

Sheriff Marge leaned back in her chair. "Okay. Walk me through your evening. Meredith, go first, since you know what's at stake."

I slid into a chair beside Pete, propped my elbows on the table, and rested my chin in a cupped hand. I closed my eyes.

I was about to prove to Pete—as if he didn't know already—why he couldn't trust me. Too many secrets. Too much jeopardy. I shouldn't have involved him—should have turned down his offer of a ride, a date. It would have been better to block him out completely, and much, much sooner. What a mess I always made of things.

I took a deep breath and started talking.

Sheriff Marge didn't interrupt until I got to the part about tackling Ferris. "Repeat that. What did he say about Ham?" Sheriff Marge pulled out her notebook.

"'Had it coming,'" I repeated. "'That pig made plenty of enemies. Should've seen his face. Coward.'" Ferris's words will be etched in my memory forever.

"And then what?"

"Then Pete hit him and, uh—he didn't talk anymore after that."

Sheriff Marge's steely gray eyes darted in Pete's direction.

"He was on top of Meredith. Hurting her," Pete said, his voice steady.

Sheriff Marge rubbed the side of her nose with her forefinger. "Continue."

I hurried through Snaggletooth's threats and helping him dive down the laundry chute. The side of my face burned under Pete's stare, but I dared not look at him.

"Let me get this straight." Sheriff Marge removed her glasses and polished them on a paper napkin. "You tipped this guy into the laundry chute by lifting him by his ankles?"

"He was already halfway hanging in the chute. His center of gravity was off—worked in my favor." I ran my finger around the rim of my coffee mug. "Four stories, counting the basement. I thought I'd killed him." I looked into Sheriff Marge's serious eyes.

"Would've been justified," Sheriff Marge muttered. "But you didn't, because he was alive and sullen when I saw him."

"He climbed back up."

"What?"

"Toeholds and knob grips. Probably the first climbing wall ever built—inside the laundry chute. It was meant as a safety feature for children playing hide-and-seek."

Sheriff Marge replaced her glasses. "So the two—Mike and Mr. Silent—they were looking for—"

"Yes." I nodded.

"Gold," Pete said.

Sheriff Marge's eyebrows shot up, and I swiveled to look at him.

Pete shrugged. "He said it. You didn't. I'll keep my mouth shut."

"Did they find it?" Sheriff Marge asked.

"No." I shook my head.

"Their truck's out back. We'll run a trace on the license, go over it for evidence. This is the break we needed to get to the next level." Sheriff Marge hunched forward. "I'll let you get home since tomorrow's another busy day. We'll lock up when we're done and secure the basement door. You can tell Pete what you need to. It's all right."

Sheriff Marge pushed her chair back, rested her hands on her thighs, and sighed.

"You need to rest, too," I said.

"Tell that to the criminals." Sheriff Marge stood and placed her mug in the sink. "Oh. I think I can also say you're no longer a suspect." She gave me a wry smile. "Yeah. I'm pretty sure about that."

I fiddled with my mug in the silence created by Sheriff Marge's absence.

Pete's chair scraped on the floor, and he stood. "Come on."

I caught sight of his extended hand out of the corner of my eye. I set down my mug and rose. Pete pulled me into his arms. I fit—my head just under his chin. He was warm, very warm. I closed my eyes.

"Those chairs won't hold two, or I'd have scooted you onto my lap," he murmured into my hair.

"I'm sorry," I whispered.

"What for?"

"For getting you in this mess—more than one mess, actually. For just assuming—"

"Hey. I make my own decisions."

"But I was a suspect—my ex-fiancé." I shuddered. "That wasn't fair to you."

"Don't argue." Pete started swaying.

I tipped my head back to see his face. "I'm not arguing—"

Pete took a step forward—straight into me—and I slid backward along with him. "Shh," he said.

Another step forward, then side, side, fast.

"Are you—dancing?"

"Shh." He raised his hand to my head and nestled my cheek against his shoulder.

I scrunched up my face and hung on, trying to keep my feet out of the way.

Pete chuckled. "You don't know how to foxtrot."

"And you do," I replied through clenched teeth.

Pete slowed. "All right. We'll save this for later. You're so tired you'd fall over if I wasn't holding you up."

"What about the gold? I want to tell you."

"Tomorrow."

"You have a job."

Pete sighed. "Yeah, I do." His head lowered until his nose rested on the top of my ear. His breath rippled across my cheek. "Call me, okay?"

"Yeah," I whispered.

Pete followed me home, all the way into the campground. He slid off the motorcycle, opened my truck door, and walked me to the RV. We stood in the circle of light cast by the yellowish fixture over the steps.

"I enjoyed riding on your bike," I said.

"Good. I'll plan a rain-check ride." He bent to pat an exuberant Tuppence, then straightened. "See you." His blue eyes sparkled.

I grinned. He really did look dashing.

He straddled the bike and pulled on his helmet.

I waved and waited until the motorcycle roar drifted down the highway before climbing the stairs with a hungry hound at my heels.

CHAPTER 19

I awoke stiff and sore. The glaring bathroom light revealed faint yellowish-green and lavender bruises on my arms and legs—and the mirror showed another bruise on my jawline. My eyes were bloodshot. Not bad for my having been in a couple of wrestling matches yesterday, but not great for a supposedly professional meeting.

I showered quickly and towel-dried my short hair. Curls sprang up, and I tried to finger-comb them in place. Rummaging in the back of a drawer produced a bottle of rarely used foundation. I smeared the beige liquid over the bruise. Not perfect, but it'd have to do. I flicked blush over my cheeks and swiped on mascara.

Brown corduroy pants and a T-shirt under a cream-colored sweater, plus loafers—the best-looking clothes I could muster for both returning my office to order and trapping a possible criminal in conversation. I grabbed a scarf to spruce up my style later, before the meeting.

Tuppence sat in the kitchen waiting for breakfast.

"Did you enjoy sleeping inside again, old girl?"

The dog thumped her tail on the hardwood floor.

I let Tuppence out and filled her bowls with dry kibble and clean water. The dog trotted around the campsite, nose to the ground.

"Any intruders in the night?"

Tuppence snorted and stuck her nose in a hole—probably a gopher hole.

"How about a hike this weekend?"

But Tuppence was too preoccupied to answer.

I returned to the warmth of the trailer and heated oatmeal in the microwave. Brown sugar, a little half-and-half, and a handful of golden raisins and chopped pecans—should keep me going for a while.

No sense dillydallying. I cringed at the thought of the condition my office had been in last night. Lots of heavy lifting to do before two p.m.

I grabbed my coat and hat and trundled down the stairs. Tuppence wasn't in sight.

"That crazy dog," I muttered. "She'd better not come home skunky again."

The truck's windshield was coated with a thin layer of feathered ice. I cranked the defroster full blast and returned to the trailer for gloves. Thanksgiving's freakish ice storm had just been the beginning. Winter would settle in for good now.

I scraped generous peepholes and backed out of the campsite.

ooo

Sheriff Marge had been as good as her word. The Imogene's front doors were locked, and everything appeared normal at the visitors' entrance. I strolled around the building and down the narrow ramp to the basement door. A sheet of plywood was screwed in place over the opening. Had the whole door been destroyed? Maybe Jim could fix it. I made a mental note to call him later.

No vehicle was parked beside the big dumpsters behind the museum; Sheriff Marge had probably already had the burglars' truck towed. How soon could the evidence be analyzed? Before Earl's appointment?

I returned to the front, let myself in, and climbed the stairs to the third floor. Early-morning light angled through the windows, illuminating stripes of wooden flooring, cross sections of banisters, and dust. The old building seemed to be sleeping. She'd had a late night, too.

A slip of paper was propped on top of the tote bag on my desk.

The boys will arrive at 8 to help restore order and reinstall cameras and microphones.
Marge.

I scooted a path through the books with my feet and stood in front of the huge picture window—one of my favorite spots. Sunlight reflected off the river's surface, turning it into a silvery mirror. Frost-coated tree limbs sparkled and sprinkled little water-drop flurries when the breeze shook them. Tiny ice flecks dusted the muddy area around the trench—which looked for all the world like a chocolate doughnut that had been rolled in granulated sugar.

My stomach growled. I groaned. Not a good sign. When I'm nervous my digestive tract goes into hyperdrive. I'd rather take on another gang of intruders than chat with Earl Rittenour.

I carefully upended the tote bag and let the contents roll onto the desk. Eight statues in thirteen pieces. Not bad considering the four-story drop. Maybe they'd landed on top of Snaggletooth instead of the other way around.

The bottom drawer of the file cabinet contains all kinds of potions and solvents for patching, cleaning, and repairing artifacts—including a bottle of super-duty wood glue. The Imogene is pretty hands-on, as museums go, and accidents sometimes happen. It's good to be able to reassure embarrassed visitors that their clumsiness is easily remedied.

I spread a large garbage bag over my desk, pushed up my sleeves, and set to work with flat toothpicks, glue, and clamps. When the statues dried, I'd touch up the fracture lines with fine-grit sandpaper and a wax filler stick. One of the benefits of having a mother who was an art therapist—I'd never been allowed to be tentative about getting my hands in dirty, smeary, messy, sticky, or greasy mediums. Diving in is always the best option.

"Express yourself," Mom had said, emphasizing the point with a big swoosh of her own hand—but she meant in finger paints, not real life. Real life for Mom is always tidy, and tightly controlled—probably overcompensation for my wildly exciting but irresponsible father, who'd abandoned us when I was three.

I'd never seen him again. My last memory regarding him was Mom slouched on the kitchen floor weeping during—and much more after—a phone call. Mom had the phone cord wrapped around her forearm and strung through her fingers like a cat's cradle while mascara ran down her face. The linoleum under Mom's bare legs—it was a hot day, and she wore cutoffs with red heart appliqués—was an orange-and-green faux-Moroccan tile pattern. It's weird, the things that stuck in my memory. And the much more important things that didn't, but that I wish had.

I heard words I didn't understand at the time—*overdose*, *addict*, *Bali*, *commune*, and *transport*. In the end his family decided to let him be buried where he'd died, halfway around the world. It would have been socially awkward to deal with the return of a crazy son/husband's body. A year later Mom married Alex, the man her family had wanted her to marry in the first place. A sure bet, Alex—reliable, on a stable career path, an upstanding member of the right socioeconomic class.

I sighed and propped up the last statue to dry, then headed to the restroom to wash the glue off my hands.

Superman and Eyebrows were coming up as I went down.

"Anything on the truck yet?" I asked.

Superman pursed his lips. "Registered to a front company in Tukwila I recognize. They're suspected of laundering money for a Somali militia group. Not on the SDN List yet, but will be soon."

"SDN List?"

"Specially Designated Nationals. Basically terrorists, drug traffickers, and their financiers with whom our government prohibits business transactions."

"And the gold?"

"Probably smuggled in to be exchanged for cash."

"But why was it stolen before it was delivered?"

Eyebrows jumped in. "It could be that Mr. Rittenour was being used without his knowledge. They may have piggybacked on his shipment."

"The shipment came from England," I said.

Superman resumed. "I'm guessing the gold was channeled from Somalia through India and into England that way. The Indians are very lax about documenting gold transactions, and England has a large Indian immigrant population—pretty easy to courier into the country. The Somali immigrant group there is small, but healthy. No doubt some of them, particularly the shadier ones, talk to one another. Unfortunately, there are always opportunists embedded among the true refugees."

"But why was the gold sent here, to Washington?"

"Probably previous ties, maybe family members. These groups have amazing networks. When it gets hot one place, they try somewhere else."

"And the statues?"

"That's what we're hoping to find out from Mr. Rittenour."

"Heard my equipment was trashed last night," Eyebrows said.

"Among other things. Go ahead—I'll be back up in a few minutes." I clomped down the remaining stairs.

Glue-free, I stopped by the gift shop. "You're early."

"Are you okay?" Lindsay hurried around the counter. "Archie said you were here last night, had a fight with—and subdued—a few burglars." She examined my face with a worried look.

"Sore and a little shook up. I'm trying not to think about how it could have turned out."

Lindsay tilted her head and peered at my jaw. "That's a nasty bruise."

I rubbed the spot gingerly. "I don't remember this happening, actually. It was kind of crazy there for a few minutes."

"Did you ice it?"

"Uh, no."

"Too late now." Lindsay shook her head. "I'm not sure it helps anyway. I just know my brothers would lie around with ice packs clutched to various body parts after football games. I always suspected it was a ploy to garner sympathy." She squeezed my arm. "I heard Pete was here, too. Some date, huh?" An impish grin played across her face.

"How *do* you hear all these things?"

"Archie called this morning while we were eating breakfast. Dad was planning to go out to Archie's place today to do soil testing—Archie's thinking about putting in a vineyard. Anyway, Archie postponed because he has to work on this case, as he called it. That's when we found out there'd been a break-in." Lindsay hooked a loose strand of hair behind her ear. "Anything I can do to help? I heard they made a mess."

"Most of my books are on the floor. I'd love help putting them back."

"You betcha." But a wrinkle creased the spot between Lindsay's eyebrows. "What were they after, Meredith? Did they steal anything?"

I wrapped an arm around the girl's shoulders. "No. They tried—but they weren't successful. I'm going to have a visitor this afternoon. After that meeting, I'll be able to tell you. Oh—" I turned and put my hands on Lindsay's shoulders. "But I can tell you one of them—" I paused and bit my lip. "I don't even know why *he* was here, but one of them was arrested for Ham's murder." I smiled into Lindsay's brown eyes. "This will all be over very soon. There's no need to worry."

To my surprise Lindsay hugged me. I guess I shouldn't have been surprised—Lindsay is an inveterate hugger. "Okay," she whispered. "If you say so."

I gave Lindsay a quick return squeeze. "Have you seen Ford this morning?"

Lindsay shook her head.

"I need to talk to him, but I'll be up in a few minutes." No need to inform Lindsay that Ford had almost had his toes shot off last night. I didn't see how Archie could have failed to mention that, but if he hadn't, I certainly wasn't going to bring it up—at least not right now.

I walked across the museum lawn to Ford's pump house turned cabin. I'd never been inside and wasn't sure if he would welcome the intrusion or be flustered by it. The door was painted glossy forest green. I knocked.

"Comin'."

Several thumps and bumps sounded inside.

I turned the knob and pushed the door open a crack. "Ford, it's just me. Please don't get up. Is it all right if I let myself in?"

But Ford was already at the door and opened it wide. "That's jes' Tommy. He's gettin' sprightly."

A small orange-and-white cat, purring much too loudly for its size, twined between Ford's feet.

I bent and scooped him up, tucking the fur ball under my chin. Tommy's purr turned squeaky.

"Ford, how are you?"

"Got nothin' to complain about."

When you get right down to it, that's true of most people, but they don't realize it. I grinned. Ford's is the kind of company worth keeping—everyone needs a good dose of cheerful perspective now and then.

"I expected you'd be on crutches."

Ford stuck his right leg out at a forty-five-degree angle and examined the toe of his boot. "These're my lucky boots, Nick said. Not supposed to be bulletproof, but the angle was jes' right. Deflected."

"Are you sore, though? Bruises?"

"Toes are purple. Nick said to rest." Ford shrugged. "Seems silly."

"Nick's training to be a medic, so he knows what he's talking about."

"I got prunin' to do." Ford's face was set, determined.

I stroked Tommy for a minute. Nothing like cuddling a contented animal to get the gray cells clicking. "You know what I've wanted for a long time?"

"Huh?"

"Tessellation puzzles for the kids who visit the museum. Mac even cut the pieces for me a year ago, and I've never had time to paint them."

"I could do that," Ford said.

"Would you? The littler kids who visit the museum would love to have something special to play with—something just for them."

Ford grinned. "I like puzzles."

"It'd be nice to have them for the winter months, especially, when the weather's not good for touring the grounds."

"Yep. Winter's comin'. Froze again last night."

"I'll bring the boxes of pieces over this afternoon. Each shape needs to be painted a different color. Think you could make time for that job in the next few days?"

"Yep. I'll clear the kitchen table." Ford turned and hobbled toward the back of the cabin.

"And prop your foot up," I called.

I snuggled my nose into Tommy's soft fur for another second, then released the cat. He trotted after Ford. Smiling, I closed the glossy green door behind me.

ooo

I paused at the top of the stairs, breathing heavily. Either last night had wiped me out more than I'd realized or I was in dire need of exercise. Or both. Shuffling sounds came from my office.

Lindsay squatted, sorting through books. The bookcases were already upright and in place along the walls.

Eyebrows, sans suit jacket, was head and shoulders into a bookcase. He backed out, a couple of long screws held between his lips and a screwdriver in hand. He waggled the screwdriver. "Not secure," he mumbled around the screws, and bent back into the bookcase, a few shelves lower.

When he emerged a minute later, lips empty, he said, "Bookcases are supposed to be affixed to the walls. You know that, right?" His bushy brows plateaued in a straight line across his forehead. "Proper safety measures." He almost clucked. "If there was an earthquake—"

"A couple of those doubled as weapons last night—for the good side." I sighed. "But of course, you're right." I didn't tell him that if there was an earthquake, the bookcases would probably be the least of my worries.

Superman blocked the doorway, holding a tub of spackle and a drywall cutout. "Best patch I can provide in short order. A little texture and paint and no one will notice."

I shook my head. "You guys go to carpenter school?"

Superman grinned, the first I'd seen. "On-the-job training. Attics, crawl spaces, vents, closets with the floorboards removed and replaced. Usually important not to let them know we've been there."

My stomach turned in knots, but I managed a tight smile. I knelt beside Lindsay.

"Any particular order?" she asked.

I pressed the heels of my palms to my forehead. "Topical, then alphabetical by author within topic. Maybe I'll draw a quick diagram." I exhaled, surveying the piles. "Yeah. Give me a few minutes."

I pulled an atlas over and grabbed a paper scrap from the file cabinet. Using the big book as a lap desk, I sketched a quick outline of each bookcase and its contents.

Lindsay looked over my shoulder. "I already found some geology books." She scooted to a neat pile, picked it up, and slid the stack into place.

By lunchtime my office was cleaner than it had ever been—bookcases no longer tipsy, books perfectly aligned, their perpendicular spines flush with the front edges of the shelves, dust vacuumed from every nook, my desk positioned in the square of sunshine filtering through the hazy window.

"Ugh." Lindsay pointed to the window and disappeared. She returned with a bottle of Windex and a roll of paper towels under her arm.

Superman fiddled with the replacement camera in the corner.

Eyebrows returned from stowing the ancient Hoover and smacked his hands together. "Looks good."

Both men were rumpled and dust-streaked.

"Hungry?" I asked. "I called Dennis Durante, one of the local vintners and caterer. He'll drop off some of his specialty sandwiches soon."

"I could go for that." Superman rubbed his forearm across his brow. "This is ready to test." He nodded at Eyebrows.

They ducked into the storage room down the hall.

"Lucky we haven't had any visitors this morning," Lindsay said. "But I'd better get back to the gift shop just in case."

"You get dibs on the sandwich you want when Dennis stops by." I wrinkled my nose and sneezed. "I had no idea it was so dirty in here."

"That's 'cause you're so focused all the time—and working. Maybe Pete'll take care of that problem." Lindsay dodged my playful poke.

"I'll come with you. I need to find those wood puzzle pieces Mac cut. They're in the basement somewhere."

I plodded down the final set of stairs and flipped on the basement light switch. Long rows of lightbulbs snapped to life, illuminating the cavernous, low-ceilinged room. One corner was cleared for photographing artifacts, set up with a digital camera, a couple of tables, spotlights, and transit carts. The rest of the room held a conglomeration of broken furniture, unlabeled collections in dusty boxes, household equipment—some working, some not. Over a century's worth of detritus.

But the puzzle pieces were from my era. They should be near the top, or front—last in, first out, right? Like the accounting method. Those technicalities had always been a little beyond me in business school—why I went into marketing instead of accounting. But when I was standing in the long room with my hands on my hips, they made sense. I was looking for cleaner, newer boxes.

I grabbed a transit cart and pushed it down the semi-clear center aisle, examining the easiest-to-reach boxes. Certain I'd labeled the puzzle pieces, I looked for black Sharpie lettering. And pounced—three neatly stacked, clean boxes labeled "squares & triangles, parallelograms, hexagons."

While I was loading the cart, the abandoned avocado-green washer-and-dryer set caught my eye. I still hadn't posted it on Craigslist. It certainly wasn't doing anyone any good in the Imogene's basement. The mansion had had industrial-size washers and dryers installed in the 1940s, back when Rupert's ancestors still hoped to produce more progeny and all live together happily in their massive vacation home. The 1970s avocado set was some kind of fluke—maybe the last servants had used it.

I wandered into the offshoot area where the laundry had been. It was directly underneath the servants' quarters upstairs—not long enough to be called a wing, just a chunky protrusion of the building. The Imogene wasn't a model of classical architecture. The mansion was a modern experiment before the idea of modern was fully developed, so from the outside it looks like something a toddler assembled with wooden alphabet blocks.

Helpfully, the last person to do laundry here had left one of the big laundry carts directly under the chute—where Snaggletooth had landed with little apparent injury. I jiggled the cart, the wheels squealing in protest.

Snaggletooth had mentioned springs. I pushed on the cart's suspended inner bottom. Springs underneath groaned and squeaked as they compressed, all the way to the cart's real bottom.

I wedged my hand between the inner bottom and the side, lifted, and peered at the springs underneath. Clever, really—it would function somewhat like a trampoline in case a kid fell down the chute.

A black rectangle lay between two coils. I squinted. A cell phone. That wasn't from the 1940s, or the 1970s.

I tipped the laundry cart on its side—a hard task. The cart was much heavier than it looked. The phone slid, and I wiggled it out.

I opened the contact list. The names weren't familiar—mostly men's first names, Mercury Trading, a couple women's names, and "Mom." There was no Earl on the list.

I handed Superman the phone when we spread out lunch on my freshly scrubbed desk. The statues had their own space on a bookshelf.

Superman flipped through the contact list, too, scowling. "Yeah, it's his. Jeff Reid—that's his real name. And Mercury Trading—that's one of the many subsidiaries of the front company the truck is registered to." He nodded and pocketed the phone. "Hopefully the information Mr. Rittenour provides will be useful in getting Mr. Reid to talk."

My stomach churned. I set my chicken salad with red onion chutney and arugula on a crusty baguette down on the parchment paper wrapper—untasted.

Eyebrows talked around a mouthful of pastrami. "The other guy, Fulmer—Ferris—whatever his name is—well, he sure blabbed. Soon as the sheriff laid out his charges, he started pointing fingers every which way. If we're lucky, Rittenour'll do the same."

"I still don't understand," I said. "Why was he here?"

"Ferris? Said he was looking for something to convert into cash 'cause he hadn't been paid. Overheard someone talking about secure display cases for valuable items. Heavy, he said. He guessed right about there being gold in the building."

I leaned back, staring at my sandwich without seeing it. So between Ford, Mac, and myself, we'd said enough for Ferris to figure it out. How many other people knew? I shook my head. It didn't matter. It'd be over soon.

I leaned forward abruptly. "I'd like you to take the gold now."

"Sure. Sure." Superman nodded. "After your meeting with Rittenour." He checked his watch. "We have a few more questions for you to ask him, and you need to have it available to show him if you need to. Yeah." He pushed away from the desk. "Let's set up."

"You mean you want the gold here?" I pointed to the statue shelf.

"Yeah. You can get it out of the safe now."

I snorted. "Some safe."

"Isn't the gold in a safe?" Superman looked worried.

I shook my head. "We don't have a safe, at least not one that works. The gold's in a dry toilet tank."

Eyebrows choked on his coffee.

Superman's mouth fell open. "You mean—they really could have walked out of here with the gold? Why didn't you—" he spluttered.

"You didn't tell me what to do with it, so I kept it where it had been. No one knew exactly where the gold was but me."

Eyebrows jumped to his feet still wiping his mouth. "I'll help you."

He followed me into the bedroom housing the chamber pot display. "Seriously," he muttered. "I understand the statues were in the laundry chute."

"I know the statues are the least valuable of the two, so that's why I led Reid there first. Especially since the wood's western hemlock," I replied.

"How'd you know that?" Eyebrows stopped in the bathroom doorway, watching me lift the tank lid.

"I know someone who knows someone." I set the lid down and tipped my head. "Microscopic analysis. They look at cell shape and density, grain patterning. I trust my source."

"And got it done faster than I ever could have." Eyebrows blew out a puff of air and looked at me with a new, open expression—relief? "We'll still have to do our own testing, confirm the results."

"Of course." I moved the gold rods to his cradled arms and replaced the lid.

CHAPTER 20

Earl arrived early, so I missed the chance for last-minute jitters.

Lindsay called while Superman and Eyebrows were doing a final audio check. "Your appointment's here." Her voice lowered to a hoarse whisper. "And I want the full scoop as soon as he leaves."

I swallowed, and my stomach reminded me that lunch was now in the garbage can. I eased down the stairs. Hesitating on the last landing, I watched, trying to size him up. Fidgety, nervous—his behavior reflected what I'd heard in his voice during our phone calls.

Earl was bald—his taut white pate mirroring the overhead lights. He wore a business suit and wing tips under a sober knee-length raincoat and paced across the parquet floor in front of the gift-shop entrance, his pant legs flapping against skinny ankles. Pivoting at the end of his picket route, he spotted me descending the stairs.

"Meredith?" He hurried over and pushed his glasses up with a forefinger against the nose piece. He extended his hand, stretching like an egret with an extraordinary wingspan.

I stepped off the last stair and tilted back to look in his face as we shook hands. "Earl."

"I expected a stack of crates—" He spun around, taking in the whole ballroom with his open arm. "Is everything all right? I drove around the building and didn't see a loading dock."

My eyebrows arched involuntarily. Nosy. I forced a smile. "Why don't you come up to my office? There's been a little—difficulty."

Earl gasped. "What?"

I took his arm and held my finger to my lips. A little tug got him headed up the stairs.

He was so melodramatic that it made playing my part easier. I'd never acted, preferring instead to help with stage and costume design in high school—again, the legacy of my art-therapist mother. Kneeling backstage among the cardboard and tempera paints had been far better than standing in front of a tittering audience trying to remember what I was supposed to say. Today the stage was my own, though—my beloved Imogene—and I felt surprisingly comfortable except for the gnawing in my midsection.

On the third floor, we passed the tightly shut storage-room door. No light seeped underneath. I imagined Eyebrows and Superman crammed in the dark, holding their breath.

From my office doorway, Earl homed in on the statues with amazing alacrity. He took three long steps to the bookcase and gingerly lifted a male statue off the shelf. Turning, he cupped the wooden figurine and held it toward the window.

"It's been broken." He said it without rancor, just an observation.

"Is that the only thing wrong with it?" I asked.

"No." Earl slowly rotated the statue, then fingered the plug I'd reglued in the bottom. "This is nothing like—I can't even call it a reproduction." He sagged and put a hand on the glass to steady himself.

I pushed a chair toward him, and he sat. I scooped the other statues off the shelf and laid them in a neat row on my desk. "Are any of them authentic?"

Earl added his statue to the row, then slumped forward, elbows on knees and face hidden in his hands. "No. No, no, no. This is not good," he mumbled.

"Earl." I put a hand on his shoulder.

As though my touch had shocked him, he jerked upright. "Where are the others? I paid for one hundred and fourteen."

"How much did you pay?"

Earl glared at me, and the light in his eyes withdrew. A secret. Did he know he'd done something illegal? His fingertips drummed on his knee and his gaze dropped.

"They were stolen." I spoke softly. "Last week. Off the delivery truck. The driver stopped here to make my delivery first, but he was attacked, knocked unconscious. They took thirteen crates but missed one, which we found and I opened."

Earl moaned. "It was too good to be true. I should have known."

I slid into my chair behind the desk and waited.

He clenched his hands on the sides of his head—as though he would have pulled out his hair if he'd had any—and doubled over, his face contorted. "I'm ruined."

"It can't be that bad."

"Oh, yes it is."

Well, if he wanted to argue, I'd take him on. "Why?"

"I spent Mona's inheritance from her grandfather on them."

I sat in stunned silence.

Earl caught the shocked look on my face. "It was the only way I could get enough money," he whined.

"What did you think you were buying? You said they're not authentic."

"Oh, it was the real thing all right." Earl's voice picked up heat. "He showed me the most detailed funerary monument I'd ever seen—and I know funerary monuments from my time in Tanzania with the Peace Corps. Said there were hundreds more. I knew they were stolen from graves, but it was a rescue. If I didn't buy them, they'd be destroyed or sold to someone who didn't understand their value." Earl stood and resumed pacing. "Those countries are all in an uproar now—there are no governments or institutions that can protect their national treasures. They're not even really nations, just warring factions. Cultural preservation is not on their list of priorities."

"Who sold them to you?"

Earl stopped and ran a hand across his forehead. "Qasim Abdul-Makir. Probably not his real name."

"And where was this?"

Earl collapsed to tie his shoe, then catapulted upright. He was like a marionette with rubber bands for strings—taut and jerky, and about to spring apart. "London. Mona'd been nagging me—wanted a big trip for our anniversary. So we went to London. She spent her time shopping, and I wandered around the museums. Some anniversary, huh? One day I got lost and ended up in, uh—well, a ghetto, really. None of the signs were in English. I stopped to ask for directions in a storefront office—desks and chairs, a few computers. I thought maybe they'd speak English. And one of them did—Qasim. He had a funerary monument on his desk. As soon as I saw it, I knew."

"Is Qasim a gallery owner? How did he get the monuments?"

"His brother-in-law runs an import/export business in central Africa."

"And robs graves?"

Earl shrugged. "Or knows someone who does."

"You made an offer to Qasim right then and there?"

"Pretty much. I mean, we talked about the monument for a while. He seemed genuinely concerned that civil war and ethnic cleansing were also destroying culturally significant artifacts. He said his brother-in-law had sent him the monument for safekeeping."

"So you arranged for a shipment."

"Yes. First to England, then here. Easier that way, Qasim said. Then he could handle all the paperwork, customs—stuff I know nothing about. All I had to do was arrange for a wire transfer to a London bank, take the cash out, and deliver it to him. I couldn't write him a check, you understand, because of the sensitive nature of the artifacts. Cash only."

"Mmm."

"But there's paperwork." Earl slid into his chair and leaned forward, suddenly eager. "Qasim gave me a receipt for the payment, and there's a contract. The goods weren't listed specifically, of course, but delivery of a shipment by October 31—it ran late—but that was documented."

"Do you have the papers with you?"

Earl shook his head. "No. In my safe at the office."

"So you knew you were buying contraband?"

"I was preserving items that otherwise would have been lost." Beads of sweat popped out all over Earl's head. He pushed his glasses up.

"How much did you pay?"

"$312,554."

"And change?"

Earl slumped. "It's all I had—all we had."

"Did you buy anything from Qasim beside the monuments?"

"No. He said if his brother-in-law came across any more monuments, he'd let me know. But he knew of one hundred and fourteen for sure. And he gave me the one on his desk. I considered it an act of good faith."

"And you keep that monument in your office at work."

Earl scowled. "How do you know?"

"I didn't think Mona would like it at home."

Earl groaned. "What am I going to tell her?"

"The truth. Let's start with the gold—what's the truth about the gold?"

"Gold?" The glasses slid up his nose as his face scrunched in confusion—a reflexive action, not faked.

I rose and pulled a gold rod off the shelf. I tried to set it lightly on my desk, but it dropped with a dull thump. Earl flinched.

"The plugs in the bottom of the monuments—each statue contained a gold rod." I perched on the edge of my chair, examining Earl's face.

He stretched out a tentative hand and touched the rod. "Is that why they were stolen?"

"Probably."

Earl's white face became sickly. The corners of his mouth stuck together when he spoke. "I'm in trouble then."

"Did you know about the gold?"

He shook his head, a barely perceptible movement, like a tremor. "What should I do?" He closed his eyes. "I'll call someone—the police, customs—who—" He raised a shaking hand and removed his glasses. "Who deals with this?"

"I do, Mr. Rittenour." Superman strode into the office and leaned over Earl. "Wayne Tubman, investigator, US Department of the Treasury." He held out his credentials and a business card.

Earl stared, blinking fast.

"Ms. Morehouse, a few minutes?" Superman tipped his head toward the door.

I pushed my chair back and scooted into the hallway. I almost bumped into Eyebrows, who was lurking just outside. He grabbed my elbow and pulled me into the storage room. We listened as Superman took Earl through a repeat of most of the questions I'd asked.

"What will happen to him?" I whispered.

"Probably not much. We'll seize all his paperwork relating to the transaction, examine his bank records, check his phone history. It sounds like he and Qasim had several back-and-forth communications. We'll try to locate this guy, Qasim. From there—" Eyebrows shrugged.

"These supply chains link up and break and re-form all the time. It's really hard to trace, but we'll do everything we can."

"But if he's telling the truth, he didn't really do anything wrong. He meant to, but since the monuments are fake, he didn't."

"Yeah." Eyebrows snorted softly. "Lucky him."

"Do you believe him?"

"Actually, I do. Body language, vocal patterns—yeah, I do. Facing his wife's probably going to be his worst punishment. And he'll never get the money back. If he was experienced, he would know not to pay more than a small deposit in advance." He peered at the video feed on a large flat-screen monitor. "That's my cue." He jumped up and hustled around the corner.

I watched as the two agents sandwiched Earl and escorted him out of my office. I quickly pushed the storage-room door closed so Earl wouldn't see me as they turned at the stair landing and descended.

When their footsteps died away, I tiptoed out of the storage room and latched the door behind me. My office felt foreign. I walked to the window and gazed at the river, my arms folded tight across my chest. I shivered, then whirled around.

The statues—and the gold—were gone.

I sighed and shook my head. I must have grown accustomed to my small, silent companions with their wooden eyes staring at me for the past several days. Even when they weren't in my office, I'd known they were close, hanging in the dark laundry chute. Gone. Probably to languish in a lonely evidence room for months or years.

And good riddance. I blew out a big breath and turned back to the window.

CHAPTER 21

Calling Pete—the moment I'd been putting off for the sheer joy of anticipation plus the more practical reason that it would be better and easier to be able to tell him the whole story instead of only part. Smiling, my fingers shaking slightly, I dialed.

A throbbing roar, the deep *wahhr-wahhr-wahhr* of the tug's diesel engines, sounded first, then Pete yelled over the noise. "Meredith."

"Are you busy?"

Loud clanking, like someone had dropped a wrench down a metal staircase. "We're linking up." He was still shouting. "Babe, I'm sorry. Can I call you back?"

Babe? Had he called me babe? I wasn't sure—all that racket. "Okay."

The line went dead.

I was in the mood for talking—which is a use-it-or-lose-it sort of thing. I dialed Arlene.

"Meredith, I was just thinking about you."

I cringed. "Good or bad?"

"Don't be silly. Good, of course. Well, not good—I mean the situation—" Arlene sighed. "I'm planning the funeral."

"When is it?"

"Friday. Several people in the prosecutor's office are pushing for a big, showy service. They want to give eulogies. I just—I don't know if I can handle that, especially—considering—"

"What do you want?"

"I want to sit in a dark room and cry my eyes out one more time. Then I want to finish separating my daffodil bulbs."

I blinked back tears. Arlene had the most beautiful garden in her neighborhood. It would certainly be a solace to her, even in winter. A way to keep busy, a way to heal.

Arlene sniffed loudly. "Enough. I keep telling myself, enough. He's not coming back." She sighed again. "Do you want to come?"

"To the funeral?" I leaned against the cool glass and held my breath. "Would it offend you if I said no? I'm not sure I can handle it, either." I bit my lip. "But I want to be there for you."

"I don't want to be there, either. I've already said good-bye. A lot of hoopla isn't going to make things better. Your stepfather offered to arrange—"

"Then let him," I interrupted. "He's good at that. Can you sneak away and visit me instead?"

Arlene laughed, a good sound. "I already have my bags packed, in my head. You have a dog, don't you? I bought a chew toy. I never look at that aisle in the grocery store. But then it just ended up in my cart."

"She'll love it. She'll love you. She's still faintly skunky, but I'll give her another bath before you come."

"Skunky?"

By the time I hung up, I'd managed to make Arlene laugh several more times by relating Tuppence's antics and Jim's turbulent repair of the ice-storm damage to my RV.

"You'd better watch out," Arlene had said. "I might just rent the campsite next to yours and never leave."

"Sounds good to me," I'd replied.

I tapped the phone against my palm, a metronome for my heart. The tension dripped from my body with each beat. I inhaled and blew a warm breath against the window glass, creating a condensation spot. It quickly evaporated.

A yellow backhoe bounced into view with one of the *Wind in the Willows* crates strapped into its wide bucket. Jim pulled to a stop. With jerky, robotic movements he angled the bucket out, over, and then into the trench. He hopped out of the cab and began unstrapping the crate.

"Knock, knock."

I spun and smiled. "How are you?"

"Homeless for a few hours. I'm letting the boys use my office to take Mr. Rittenour's statement," Sheriff Marge said.

"Any leads on where the stolen crates are?"

"Treasury raided the front company in Tukwila a couple hours ago—the one the truck's registered to. They were there. One hundred and six statues."

"And one hundred and six kilograms of gold?"

"Yep. Agent Tubman thinks the proceeds were meant to fund an energy source for a Somali warlord."

"Energy?"

"Their economy's shattered. Out in the bush, if you need electricity for a military compound, where does it come from? The country probably has untapped natural gas reserves, but that would take a lot of research and drilling. And none of the militias can offer the security necessary for the length of time it would take to get a facility productive, not to mention international sanctions that make that kind of investment next to impossible. Tubman thinks it might be as simple as methane."

I wrinkled my nose.

"I guess they have a lot of goats and cows," Sheriff Marge said.

"Regarding the other matter, one of the boys mentioned that Ferris—uh, Fulmer, was pointing fingers." I raised my eyebrows.

Sheriff Marge sighed. "I don't like it, but we'll have to investigate his allegation."

"Which is?"

"That a woman named Anita Hadley promised to pay him fifty thousand dollars if he killed Ham."

I pursed my lips in a silent whistle. "Anita? She's his opponent—for the Superior Court seat. She also has other reasons—like Val and me—not to think fondly of Ham. But she offered to *pay*?"

"She got cold feet or something, probably when she found out he'd actually done it, and reneged. Being tight for cash, he decided to come back and lift the valuables he'd heard were at the Imogene while he figured out a way to force her to pay. Expected it would be a one-night deal, so he wouldn't have to show his face in town again."

"Whoa." I shook my head. "That seat's going unfilled."

"You sound as though you're sure she did it."

"I know Anita. A viper in a pit of snakes." I wrinkled my nose. "Well, you know what I mean. She can be vicious. With words, anyway. Had a reputation in the PA's office."

Sheriff Marge grunted.

"You know," I continued, "she assisted Ham with the Ozzie Fulmer trial. Maybe that's how she met Ferris."

Sheriff Marge pulled out her phone. "'Bout time I called Clark County."

I gazed out the window and listened to Sheriff Marge run through Ferris's crimes with her counterpart. It sounded as though Anita would be brought in for questioning ASAP.

Jim was making tracks. Three crates in the trench already. The grass would grow back in the spring, in plenty of time to be cool and inviting for summer picnics. Birds singing, the omnipresent breeze rippling the edges of colorful blankets, baskets of food and jugs of lemonade. My perfect world. Nope, one more thing—Pete on one of those blankets. *That* would be perfect.

Sheriff Marge hung up and sighed. "I'm afraid it's going to be he-said, she-said with Ms. Hadley. Unless Fulmer can produce proof of a deposit."

"Or witnesses to their conversations. Phone records?"

"Mmm." Sheriff Marge nodded.

Lindsay's head popped through the doorway. "Can I come in? I'm bursting." The girl was actually hopping.

I laughed. "Out with it."

"I got in! Accepted! Oh, thank you." Lindsay squeezed Sheriff Marge, knocking her glasses askew.

Sheriff Marge huffed.

"So soon? That must be a speed record. They knew they had to snatch you up fast so some other school wouldn't get you." I sashayed around my desk and hugged Lindsay. "Congratulations."

Lindsay's smile faded. "But it means I'll be leaving in January. I could work summers if you want me, but—" She let out a little whimper.

"Don't worry about that. And of course I want you—are you kidding? Summer's our busiest time. We'll definitely need you. We'll find a temporary replacement, just while you're at school." I patted Lindsay's shoulder. "Have you told your parents and Greg yet?"

"No. I just got the e-mail." Lindsay rebounded with a squeal. "I'll call them." She darted from the room.

I plopped in my chair and shot a wry glance at Sheriff Marge. "Not even my kid, but I feel like a baby just flew the nest."

"It's called aging. Pretty soon you'll start getting weepy when you see a kid learning to ride a bicycle or drive a car, or getting married. And it doesn't matter whose kid it is."

"You do that?"

Sheriff Marge waved her hand dismissively. But then she said, "Hallie, Ben's wife, is pregnant."

Lindsay had already broken the ice, so I jumped up and gave Sheriff Marge another squeeze. "Your first grandchild!"

Sheriff Marge chuckled and wiped the corner of her eye. "Maybe I should learn to knit."

After Sheriff Marge left, I wandered outside to check on Jim's progress up close. He was in the trench, back to me, shoveling. I was almost within greeting range when my phone rang.

"Hey there."

"Sorry about earlier," Pete said.

"No worries. I don't want you distracted when you're operating cables and winches and stuff. I like you all in one piece." I veered away from Jim and the trench, heading for the riverbank.

"Me, too. How are you?"

"Relieved. It's over. The gold's safe with the US Treasury Department, and Ham's killer—you met him last night, Ferris—has more or less admitted to the murder."

"So you're a free woman."

I chuckled. "So to speak. How long will you be gone?"

"A week—ten days, maybe. I have another job lined up after this one."

I sank onto a boulder, letting my feet dangle a few inches above the water.

"You're quiet," Pete said. "Miss me already?"

I smiled. "Yes, I do. Already."

"Good." A steady thrumming filled the line, as though Pete had moved closer to the tug's engines. It was a rhythmic sound—lulling, like the river itself.

"Are you dreaming again?" Pete asked.

"Hmm?"

"A few days ago, when you had a quiet pause, you said you were dreaming."

"Oh, that." I wrinkled my nose. "I suppose it's better if some things stay inside my head."

"We're going to have to work on that, because I'm very interested in what goes on in there. Are you going to let me in on your thoughts?"

I gazed at the new winking lights on the Oregon shore—semitruck headlights in the early dusk, traveling east on I-84. The breeze lifted a curl, and it tickled my cheek.

I closed my eyes. "Yes."

SNEAK PEEK

SIGHT SHOT

An Imogene Museum Mystery
Book 3

When asked to research old documents for a local family, Meredith Morehouse, curator of the eclectic Imogene Museum, jumps at the chance. As if she didn't already have enough to do—hiring a new gift shop manager, keeping tabs on Rupert Hagg, the museum director, who may have been hoodwinked by a woman Meredith suspects is after his money; not to mention finding time to see Pete Sills, the hunky tugboat captain she's just started dating.

Then Meredith's investigation unearths hints that a decade-old suicide might not have been suicide after all. So many secrets in the small, riverside town of Platts Landing, Washington. Will someone kill again to preserve a secret?

1

I plopped into my chair, then froze, hands hovering over the keyboard. After two years as curator of the Imogene Museum, I know all her noises—old building noises—creaks and clacks, the moan and rattle of loose wood-framed windows, floorboards squeaking as they settle deeper on rusty nails.

This was a new noise. Regular, but not so regular as to be mechanical. I held my breath. The sound rose in volume—softly, louder, gurgle, gurgle—then died.

I counted slowly to fifteen. There it was again—pitching up at the end as though ratcheting into a higher gear.

Did I mention I'd unlocked the front doors myself, and locked them again behind me? I was supposed to be alone in the old mansion, at least until the new cashier/gift-shop attendant, Edna Garman, arrived at nine forty-five to prepare the museum for its ten o'clock opening.

I quickly scanned my office for some means of protection. Where's a baseball bat when you need one? I settled for an old map tube. Flimsy, but four feet long.

I tiptoed out of my office and waited, listening hard.

Gkgkgkawkaw tchkaw gork shhheww.

I cocked my head. Where was it coming from?

The Imogene has so many nooks and crannies and hard surfaces—lath and plaster walls, oak floors, stairs and banisters. The sound bounced and ricocheted, but it was too muffled to be on the third floor.

I sneaked down the stairs one step at a time, avoiding the creaky spots.

Gkgkgkawkaw tchkaw gork shhheww splack eeeka squeeeeak, sigh.

My heart thumped faster. The last few notes had definitely been the sound of squeaky springs in an old mattress.

The only bed in the mansion's fourteen bedrooms is in the chamber pot display room on the second floor. I hugged the wall and inched down the hallway.

The door to the chamber pot exhibit was open a few inches. I clung to the doorframe and slid sideways until I had an eye at the opening. Two swaddled forms lay on the bed.

I slid a little farther. One of the forms was topped with disheveled white hair. The other head was bald and shiny, with a bulbous nose protruding above the sheet.

I should have expected it, but I hadn't.

Gkgkgkawkaw tchkaw gork shhheww.

I jumped and dropped the map case. It clattered on the floor.

One eye in the bald head popped open.

I pushed the door open halfway and managed a wobbly smile.

His other eye popped open. "Good morning. We were wondering when someone would let us out." The man sat up, revealing a white sleeveless T-shirt and fuzzy-haired shoulders, and patted his companion. "Ginny, wake up."

Ginny moaned and rolled over, her back to him.

The man winked at me and pinched Ginny's bottom through the blankets. Ginny grunted and slapped his hand away.

I grew warm, and I think the color of my face may have matched that of the gaudy pink roses on the Victorian transferware chamber pot in the nearest display case. I was suddenly mesmerized by a crack between the floorboards.

"Who'd have thought we'd spend our anniversary locked in a museum?" the man said. "We have to put this in our New Year's letter to family and friends."

My jaw dropped while my mind scrambled over itself trying to work out the implications of his statement. Locked in the museum? Overnight? A PR nightmare, not to mention the anxiety and discomfort they must have experienced.

My hand flew to my mouth. "I—I'm awfully sorry."

"Great adventure," the man said. "You're a pretty little thing. Who are you?"

"M—Meredith Morehouse. Curator. Oh, I am so sorry." I stepped closer, then thought better of it. Maybe they needed some privacy to make themselves presentable. "I'll just, uh, I'll wait in the hall. When you're ready, I'll let you out. But I—I'd like to know how this happened." I backed out of the room, closing the door behind me.

I leaned against the wall and chewed my lip. Ginny and the man talked in low tones on the other side of the door. There was shuffling and bumping, then Ginny giggled. Maybe they weren't angry—oh, how I hoped they weren't angry. What a dreadful mistake.

The man cracked the door open and stuck his head out. "Ah, yes. We're ready. I'm Wallace." He stepped into the hall, hand in hand with Ginny. "And this is my bride of fifty-two years, Virginia."

I grinned. "Congratulations."

Ginny touched my arm. "You're a dear. Did we startle you? Wally snores like the dickens."

I shook my head and smiled at Wally. "It's good you do. Otherwise I wouldn't have known you were here. I'm so glad you found the bed and blankets to keep warm. What happened?"

"Well, we knew we were late," Ginny said. "But Wally really wanted to see the model cannon collection. He collects them, too, you know."

"Always been interested in anything that goes *boom*," Wally interrupted, loudly.

"So we tried to hurry and thought there'd be an announcement. You know, 'The museum will be closing in five minutes'—something like that. Then all of a sudden, the lights went out. All of them. We ran back through the ballroom—well, as fast as we can run at our age." Ginny laughed. "The glass doors were locked, and the only car in the parking lot, besides ours—a light-blue Volkswagen Beetle—was pulling away. We waved and pounded on the doors, but I'm not surprised she didn't hear us."

"We looked for a phone but couldn't find one, and we'd left ours in the car," Wally said. "Thought maybe there was one in the gift shop, but those doors were locked, too."

I nodded. The museum's two landline phones are in the gift shop and my office, which are both routinely locked when not occupied.

"I am so sorry." I exhaled. "I know I can't make this up to you."

"No need." Wally's laugh boomed, too. "Bet none of our friends can top this." He supported his jiggling belly with both hands.

"I'm embarrassed. We don't normally treat our visitors this way."

"Not to worry, dear," Ginny said. "We were quite comfortable. We were going to stay in a hotel anyway."

I rubbed my forehead, then tried to pat down my hair. My unmanageable brown curls were probably standing on end from the shock. "Are you hungry? I have a friend who owns a winery and bistro just a few miles down State Route 14. I'd like to call him and arrange brunch for you. And I insist on having the museum pick up the tab—part of our bed-and-breakfast package." I smiled, hoping they'd catch my joke.

"What do you think?" Wally turned to his wife.

Ginny leaned in and pecked his cheek. "Sounds lovely."

I escorted them to the entrance and gave them directions to the Willow Oaks tasting room. I also asked for their phone number and tapped it into my phone's contact list. I'd call later and apologize again.

They drove away in the tan sedan I'd parked my pickup next to. I relocked the doors.

It's not unusual for people to leave their cars in the large parking lot shared by the Imogene Museum and the county park and marina. And Wally and Ginny's car had Washington plates, so I hadn't thought much of it. But from now on, I would treat any car left after hours as cause for inquiry.

And the light-blue Beetle seen leaving last night? I clenched my fists. Edna Garman's.

I'd fired two people at my old job as a director of marketing. One for failure to appear, and one for pilfering. Never for incompetence. I wished I'd slept in.

ooo

I'd hired Edna because I was desperate and because she was boring. So boring that I felt sorry for her. I figured minding the gift shop would spice up her life. It had not occurred to me that I should check if she knew how to count, add, and subtract.

I was desperate because Lindsay Smith, our longtime gift shop manager, was going off to college in the middle of January. I'd run ads and posted flyers for the position, but received little interest over the Christmas holiday.

Finally Edna called. She had arrived on time for her interview, dressed in tan pants that matched her stiff, shoulder-length hair and a pale-blue shirt that matched her eyes. A slender, drab woman in her thirties.

I'd asked Edna about art-related hobbies and interest in local history and Columbia River Gorge geology—the subjects our visitors usually inquire about. She answered most questions with negative monosyllables, but she did say she liked to draw. She lived with her mother, an arrangement that seemed mutually agreeable, and she had a driver's license and a Social Security number. She had some experience cashiering at a pet store that had since closed. I thought— hoped—that she just needed some outside stimulus. I was looking forward to watching her personality emerge. Some people don't interview well.

Now, two days into the job, she'd failed to tally how many visitors had entered and left the museum and verify that the building was empty before locking up—a responsibility I had reviewed with her. Maybe we were just lucky all our visitors had departed on time the first day.

I paced the ballroom inside the museum's double-door entrance, watching for Edna's Beetle. The sooner I got this over with, the better for both of us.

Maybe I'd skimmed over the tallying concept too quickly for Edna. Maybe she'd been too shy to tell me she didn't understand. I hurried into the gift shop and pulled the spiral-bound notebook from under the cash register. It was open to the place where I'd written "Thursday, December 28" and drawn two columns labeled "in" and "out." There were no hash marks for Thursday, and no notation of Friday. The rest of the page and a dozen pages following were filled with doodles—cats, mostly—and butterflies.

Oh, no.

I popped open the cash register and was grateful to see that the drawer wasn't empty. The usual scanty selection of bills and coins occupied the compartments. I should have monitored Edna more closely. I'd become accustomed to Lindsay's efficiency and was too immersed in my own work.

Pounding rattled the front doors. My sweat glands went into overdrive, and I swallowed. What should I say to her?

More pounding. Then I realized that if Edna had arrived, she would have let herself in with the set of keys I'd given her.

I tucked the notebook under my arm, hopped off the stool, and scooted around the counter. A burly man in an olive-green canvas field jacket, jeans, and boots waved and pointed to the crash bar on the glass door. He mouthed the words, "Could you open early?"

We don't usually have people beating down the doors to see the Imogene's eclectic exhibits, but I appreciate visitors who are enthusiastic about our artifacts. I unlocked the doors and pushed one open for him.

"Saw the lights on. I'm tight for time," the man said. His dark-blond hair was cut military-short, and he had a mustache and goatee trimmed around thick, fleshy lips. He carried a beat-up leather valise, as large as a carpetbag and crinkled with age.

"No problem. Is there an exhibit you're particularly interested in? I can show you where it is."

"No, thanks." He shifted the valise to his left hand and stuck out his right. "I'm Wade Snead. Was wondering if you'd take a look at some family papers. See if there's anything of value."

I shook his hand. "Meredith Morehouse. Curator. But it sounds like you need to talk to a document appraiser. I could give you a few names."

"We're a local family. Figured you'd have archives to compare against." He held the valise toward me, shaking it a little the way you'd tease a dog with a bacon strip.

Okay, so maybe I was salivating. "I'm not qualified. I could do some research, but I couldn't assign value—at least not officially."

"Whatever you can do would be great. I have to go out of the country for a few days—"

"Oh!" I said, accidentally cutting Wade off.

Edna had sneaked in. There's no better word for it. And she was standing just behind and to the right of Wade, her face pinched. She looked me up and down, took in the notebook under my arm, and squinted. Two bright-pink spots appeared on her cheeks. "I quit!" she yelled.

Wade whirled around, and we both stared at her.

I opened my mouth, closed it, opened it again. "Okay." I nodded. "In fact, that's fantastic."

"You—you can't just—" Edna's hands tightened into fists, one of which held the museum key ring. "I'll sue!" She launched toward me.

I gasped and stumbled backward. It took a second to realize that while Edna's arms and legs were moving, she wasn't going anywhere. My heartbeat raced in my ears.

"Let me go!"

"No." Wade frowned. "You need to think about this."

"You—" Edna swiveled and tried to kick Wade's shins.

He shifted his grip from her coat collar to her shoulders and held her in a stiff-arm block. She flailed ineffectually, turning redder by the moment.

"You should leave," Wade said.

I jumped forward, holding a finger in the air. "Just a minute. I need the keys."

Edna suddenly went stiff and locked her arms behind her back. She fixed me with a vicious glare.

"I'll trade." I flipped the pages of the notebook. "Your drawings for my keys."

Her eyes darted back and forth as she considered. Then her hand jutted forward, her knuckles white around the keys.

I advanced slowly.

She lunged for the notebook, but I pulled it back.

"Keys." I held my other hand out, palm up.

She dropped the keys in my palm and snatched the notebook. She backed up, clutching it to her chest, then turned and barged through the front doors. The Beetle's tires squealed on the pavement as she sped away.

I exhaled. The keys in my hand jangled from my shaking. I stuffed them in my jeans pocket.

Wade chuckled.

I turned to him. "You know Edna?"

"Went to high school together. Hasn't changed much." He ran a hand through his short hair. "Always was an odd bird."

"Thanks for restraining her."

Wade stooped, picked up the valise, and handed it to me, his eyebrows raised in a question. "So we're even?"

I wrapped my arms around the bag and hugged it, surprised by its heft. "Sure." I grinned. "Phone number? Way I can contact you?"

Wade pulled a wallet out of his back pocket and extracted a business card. "Phone, e-mail—it's all there. Appreciate it." He tucked the card between my fingers.

Wade left the museum and climbed into his muddy Dodge Ram pickup. A big truck for a big guy.

And a big bag. I let it slide to the floor. "Whew." I flipped his card over. It read "Wade Snead, Owner & Contractor, Snead HVAC," and the phone number had an area code I didn't recognize.

I hauled Wade's bag up to my office, then hustled back downstairs to officially open the museum. I'd have to pull gift-shop duty today and put all research on hold until I could find a replacement for Edna.

NOTES

The Imogene Museum mystery series is a tribute to the Columbia River Gorge and the hearty people who live in gorge towns on both sides of the Oregon/Washington border. It's an extraordinary piece of God's real estate, and I savor driving, sightseeing, picnicking, and camping along its entire length. Hitching a ride on a tug run from Umatilla to Astoria is on my bucket list.

If you're familiar with the area, you may realize that I've taken liberties with distances in some cases. Mostly I squished locations (albeit fictional) closer together to move the story along and also to showcase the amazing geologic and topographic features of the gorge. In real life for many gorge residents, the round trip to a Costco or a bona fide sit-down restaurant might well take a full day. This kind of travel time isn't helpful when you're chasing a fleeing murderer. But, if you're not Sheriff Marge and have time to enjoy the scenery, the gorge is spectacular, and I encourage you to come experience it for yourself.

However, please don't expect to actually meet any of the characters in this book. All are purely fictional, and if you think they might represent anyone you know, you're mistaken. Really. I couldn't get away with that.

ACKNOWLEDGMENTS

Profound thanks to the following people who gave their time and expertise to assist in the writing of this book:

The wise, good-humored, and eagle-eyed ladies in my writing critique group—Diane Cammer, Sandy Stark, Anne Taylor, and Karen Williams.

My insightful beta readers—Debra Biaggi, Sharon Freiwald, and BJ Thompson.

Sergeant Fred Neiman Sr. and all the instructors of the Clark County Sheriff's Citizen's Academy. The highlights had to be firing the Thompson submachine gun and stepping into the medical examiner's walk-in cooler. Oh, and the K-9 demonstration and the officer survival/lethal force decision-making test. And the drug task-force presentation with identification color spectrum pictures and the—you get the idea.

I claim all errors, whether accidental or intentional, solely as my own.

ABOUT THE AUTHOR

Photo © 2012 Sarah Milhollin

I live in a small town in the west end of the Columbia River Gorge. When I grow up, I fully intend to be a feisty old lady. In the meantime, I regularly max out my library's lending limit and have happily declared a truce with the clover in the lawn, but am fanatical about sealing up cracks in my old house, armed with a caulking gun. Due to the number of gaps I have yet to locate, however, I've also perfected my big-spider shriek.

I love wool socks, Pink Lady apples with crunchy peanut butter, scenery of breathtaking grandeur, and weather just cool enough to require a sweater—all of which are plentiful in the Pacific Northwest. I am eternally grateful to have escaped the corporate world with its relentless, mind-numbing meetings and now write (or doodle or fantasize or cogitate or stare out the window or whatever you want to call it) full-time.

I post updates on my website, www.jerushajones.com.

If you'd like to be notified about new book releases, please visit my website to sign up for my e-mail newsletter. Your e-mail address will never be shared, and you can unsubscribe at any time.

I love hearing from readers at jerusha@jerushajones.com.